waiting
to
dive

Also by Karen Rivers

Barely Hanging On

The Actual Total Truth

Karen Rivers

waiting
to
dive

Scholastic Canada Ltd.
Toronto New York London Auckland Sydney
Mexico City New Delhi Hong Kong Buenos Aires

Scholastic Canada Ltd.
604 King Street West, Toronto, Ontario M5V 1E1, Canada

Scholastic Inc.
557 Broadway, New York, NY 10012, USA

Scholastic Australia Pty Limited
PO Box 579, Gosford, NSW 2250, Australia

Scholastic New Zealand Limited
Private Bag 94407, Greenmount, Auckland, New Zealand

Scholastic Children's Books
Euston House, 24 Eversholt Street,
London NW1 1DB, UK

Cover photo by Rodrigo Moreno

Library and Archives Canada Cataloguing in Publication

Rivers, Karen, 1970-
Waiting to dive / Karen Rivers.

ISBN 978-0-439-93824-2

I. Title.
PS8585.I8778W34 2007   jC813'.54   C2006-906732-5

6 5 4 3 2 1   Printed in Canada   07 08 09 10 11

To Torin, Natasha, Matthew, Tristan, Owen and Linden; and to all the other past, present and future island kids.
— *K.R.*

chapter 1

Under my feet, the grey rock is hot and gritty, and nasty white barnacles scratch at my toes. Barnacle cuts are the worst, of course, because they have something close to a million little teeth on the tops of them and when they cut your skin, oooh boy. They take forever to heal. The rock is sandstone, which, as I'm sure you know, is sand that has baked in the sun for an incredibly long time, like a thousand years or a hundred. The hot, hot sun is like the kiln at school where Mrs. Taylor fires our clay ashtrays, turning them from grey mud into something different, more like china. Maybe in another fifty years or so this rock will turn into something like that, something shinier and smoother.

Mrs. Taylor. Hmmph. Only two more weeks of Mrs. Taylor and then school is out for summer. I can't say that I'll miss old Mrs. Taylor, or that I won't. She's okay, as teachers go. She isn't even that old, probably. She is not as old as my mum or anything. Still, in September, I'll be in Grade Five, and that will be that. No more Grade Four. No more Mrs. Taylor.

I've been standing here for a long time. Every once in a while one of the dogs comes over and sniffs at me, as if to say, "Dive already!" So I throw them a stick, and the big dog goes and gets it, belly-flopping into the water, while the puppy just sits there and looks happy. He's panting like crazy because he's so hot, but he stays there anyway. His tongue is bright pink and drippy, like a cherry popsicle. I'll tell you more about the dogs in a minute. I mean, they're a whole story on their own.

It's hot in the sun. I'm practically melting myself; little dribs of sweat are mixing in with the suntan stuff that stinks like coconut, which is just fine if you live in, say, Hawaii, but smells wrong here at the cabin where the water is dark green and the trees aren't made of palm but are tall, sticky Douglas firs that leak gluey drops of sap. I'm standing here, staring at the water, which, like I said, is dark green, not that pretty light blue you get in Hawaii. And I know that's true because I've been there. Also, here there is a lot of junky stuff floating on the surface in front of me. Seaweed and little bits of wood and rubbish that the tide has brought in. At the same time, the water looks cold and good, like it's inviting me to swim. I could just jump in. But I won't.

Some of the seaweed that I can see is that brown stuff with the little bubbles on it that pop when you squeeze them, like the bubble plastic that you can wrap really precious gifts in before you send them through the mail. Bladder wack, I think it's called, or maybe bladder wrack. The seaweed, not the mailing stuff. Also, there is kelp, which you can pop, too, only it has to be a little bit dry, and then you can put it on a rock and jump on it. Sometimes it sounds like a balloon popping. Usually, with the kelp, I try to find a really big one that is fresh and not dry, and then I use my penknife to carve a little face on it. The long weedy part looks like hair — you can even cut holes in the stem part and put in sticks for arms and legs, making a perfectly good kelp doll. They don't last very long. I tried to keep one once, but after a small while, like an hour, it started to stink and Mum made me throw it out.

There are no other kids here this weekend, even though it's a hot, perfect, almost-summer week-end in the beginning of June. I mean, I know it's not summer yet, but who cares? The sky is super blue, with these white streaky clouds, like melting ice cream. I wish I could have ice cream right now, but it's way back in the cabin through the woods and it's too far to go by myself. My feet hurt from the bumpy rock.

"Just jump in!" Mum calls.

"No!" I answer. I don't tell her that I can't jump. That I don't want to jump, because I want to dive. I'm just waiting for the dive to come into me, so that suddenly I'll know how to fly off the rock with pointed toes and slip into the water without splashing. Like a ballerina. I know it can happen, because that's how I learned to cartwheel. I just waited, and then, all of a sudden, my arms and legs knew exactly what to do. I could feel it. I'm really good at that stuff — cartwheels and walkovers and handstands. I take gymnastics after school in this big old gym downtown with a bunch of other kids. It's always dusty in there from all the chalk dust, and it makes me sneeze. I like the chalk, though; it's the best part, stepping up to the bar and rubbing chalk on your hands to stop your sweat from sliming up the wood and making you drop off. Actually, to tell you the honest to Pete truth, I don't really like the parallel bars. They give me bruises on my hips.

Maybe I do like them. I don't like the bruises, but I like the feeling of flying, and the spinning, and the chalk. Like I said, the chalk is the most fun.

Anyway, now I'm waiting for the dive.

My legs are itchy. They are covered with a million mosquito bites that are baking in the sun. I try not to scratch them because I once scratched so hard that I scratched one right off and it bled like crazy. I could have bled to death. I'm serious. It was horrendously awful. That happened when I was a little kid — maybe three years ago, or four. Now I'm ten already, so I'm old enough to know better. Or at least, that's what Mum would say.

I still have a scar from that old mosquito bite. I remember it really well. The bleeding and the itching. It happened when we used to come up here with my Real Dad. I don't really want to talk about him, but I thought I should mention this one thing, in case you were wondering: my Real Dad is dead. He died when I was almost seven. I say that so you know, that's all. So don't ask me about it.

The sun is dipping a little bit behind the trees, so there are big black shadows on the water. The tide keeps coming in, and pretty soon I'll be standing here on an island, instead of a rock. Then, I guess, I'll have to jump in and swim to shore. I practise swinging my arms around and up. It feels almost right. Around and up. I bend my knees a little and bounce up and down. Diving is probably a whole lot easier on those springy boards like they have at the pool. This rock, let me tell you, is not very springy. It's just a big hot lump of dead sand waiting around in the sun to become something fancier.

I can see that Mum and my New Dad are packing up the kids' toys and junk, and I can tell that any second they are going to start yelling about going back to the cabin for supper, and I'm a little bit mad, because I have wasted all afternoon standing on this rock instead of fooling around on my raft, or practising underwater handstands. And we have to leave in the morning because there is school on Monday, so I won't have another chance.

One of the kids is crying. I think it's Marly. She's not really my sister, not even a half-sister. She came with my New Dad. That should be obvious. I mean, my name is Carly. If she was my real sister, would they have called her Marly? How stupid does that sound? We only have her on weekends. She's four, but you wouldn't know it; she's totally a baby. A crybaby. I might as well be honest here and say that I don't really care too much for Marly. Mealy Marly is how I think of her.

She's like a mealy little worm or something, all skinny and wild and drooly. Her brother, Shane, is only two. "Two going on twenty," Mum says. He's like this little tiny old man when he talks. He says some really strange grown-up things in his little baby voice. He's cute — cuter than Marly, anyway. She has freckles — a million billion freckles — and bright red hair. They should have called her Annie, like Little Orphan Annie. Shane is more like my New Dad, really dark curly hair and skin that is so white it's almost greenish-white, and big brown eyes. My New Dad's first wife was a redhead. She isn't dead. She just didn't want to live in his house anymore, particularly right after Shane was born. Maybe he cried too much and kept her awake, I don't know. My New Dad must have really loved that house because he stayed and she went to live somewhere else. I've seen her apartment. I can tell you one thing — it's no great shakes, either. The house is five million times nicer. Whatever. "To each his own," my mum says. Although the apartment has this one neat thing, which is the elevator that takes you up to her floor. It has mirrored walls and purple carpet. I love purple. If I was allowed, I'd paint my whole room purple. Dark purple, light purple, lavender, pink-purple, all the different purples.

The water is starting to tickle at my toes, which are painted, of course, with this purple-red colour called Toast of New York. My mum only lets me paint my toes, because she says I am too young to paint my fingers. Whatever. Like if I painted my fingers, people might mistake me for a grown-up and I would have to stop going to school and get a job and have babies and get married a few times. Forget it. It makes me mad, to tell you the truth. But I won't say anything. That's the kind of mad I get. Sort of a bubbling inside kind of mad that I keep down by swallowing hard and squinting at a really bright light. It works perfectly. You should try it. Really — I mean it. Just thinking about the fingernail polish is starting to get my madness percolating a little bit, and I stare up at the sun with squinty eyes. The spots of grey and white cool my madness right down to nothing, down to a little snowflake of madness that melts and goes away.

I really have to hurry. The sun is sinking like a stone. I look at the water, which is shiny and smooth like a mirror, or, at least, like a mirror with a bunch of junk floating in it.

And I close my eyes.

And swing my arms.

And spring forward.

And . . .

It doesn't really work. I sort of just tip over into the water, which smacks against my belly with a solid *thwack*. I can tell you, that stings. For one thing, it takes me about a minute to get my breath back. And my skin goes all red in the space between my bikini top and bottom. This is my favourite bathing suit of all time — it's really light blue with white and yellow daisies.

Anyway.

I kind of fool around in the water a bit. I mean, I'm here now, so I might as well. I wish there were other kids to play with, real kids, I mean. My age. But I'll have to play with the dogs instead. I should tell you about them. There're two of them, but you already know that. An old one, and a young one. Roo, that's the old one, used to be my Real Dad's. She's huge. I mean it — she weighs more than I do. She is like a big, white bear. She is partly malamute and partly lab. I think her mum was a lab and her dad was a malamute. Or maybe it's the other way around. Whatever. She has this long hair that gets super heavy in the water. Also, her claws are too sharp, so she isn't really any good to swim with. Well, that doesn't stop her. She just jumps right in after me and swims around in big circles. There is something funny about her when she's swimming. She looks like she can't wait to get out, but also that she can't leave me here alone. Kind of panicked, which, to tell you the truth, makes me feel sort of good. She loves me a lot. Maybe a little bit in the same way that my Real Dad did. But enough about that.

The puppy — my puppy — is still just standing on the rock, which is now an island, just like I said it would be. His name is Blue. So we have Roo and Blue, more rhyming names. Stupid, don't you think? Blue is mine. I named him a rhyming name on purpose, so that everyone could see how dumb it sounded. Marly, Carly. Roo, Blue. It didn't really work. Everyone just said it was a super-cute name. Huh. Mum and my New Dad gave Blue to me for my tenth birthday. I think it's so I won't feel left out or something, or sad about my Real Dad, or mad that they got married and that I have to share everything with Marly and Shane. Whatever. He's really cute, like a little brown bug — Blue, that is. My little buggy wuggy. We don't know what he is — he came from the animal shelter — or how big he'll get. But right now he's just the right size, small enough for me to carry around. My New Dad says he's partly poodle, but I don't believe him. He thinks he knows everything. I think Blue looks like a very small curly wolf, and maybe he is just a little bit wild. Mum says he's more like some kind of fancy water dog than anything else, but he does have those pointy wolf ears. I guess I don't care. I love him just the same.

I hope he can figure out how to swim to shore. I mean, I don't think I can carry him and swim at the same time, even though he's not very big.

I turn a few somersaults underwater, holding my nose so the water doesn't burn it inside. It's just the worst when salt water gets in your nose, and then trickles down the back of your throat. I mean, think about it — how disgusting is that? It's like nose drops, which I also strongly hate. Roo is still swimming around me in big circles, looking more and more tired by the minute. I feel kind of bad about that, so I decide to go in and let her rest.

I swim back to the rock and try to lure Blue into the water. "Come on, baby," I coo sweetly. "Come to mummy."

Of course, he's a dog, so I guess he's not that bright. He just stands there and wags his tail and sniffs at the water, which, might I add, is now almost covering his whole little island. He takes a little lick of it, and makes a face. Obviously it tastes bad to dogs, too.

Actually, the water is getting kind of cold, and to tell you the truth, I am not crazy about the tree shadows. The black water is sort of spooky, and it is getting pretty deep. At least over my head about ten times. I mean, if there were ten of me I could just stand on my shoulders on my shoulders on my shoulders ten times and still be able to breathe. But that is not the case here, and I am an excellent swimmer but don't relish the thought of swimming with a puppy under my arm, and Roo looks about ready to drown. I wouldn't be able to pull her up. She weighs way too much. I'd probably sink, for sure, and then where would we be? Under all that green water, not able to breathe. That would be a fine toodle-oo.

I have to do what I have to do, I guess. I swim really close and reach out to Blue and grab his collar, which has pictures of Scooby-Doo all over it, and just pull him into the water.

Splash!

He sort of sinks for a second with this scared look, like he thinks I'm really mean, and his little head goes under. But then he just bobs back up again, and starts flapping and swimming towards the beach. It must look funny, one girl, one puppy and one tired, huge dog, all swimming as fast as they can to the shore. Actually, Blue gets there first, before me. He's a really good swimmer. He just had to wait a while for the swimming to come into him, then he knew how. Just like that.

I just wish I'd waited a little longer myself. Maybe the dive would have come. Just maybe.

chapter 2

"Blue, sit! Sit, Blue!"

He just stares at me with his cute puppy eyes. "Come on, Blue, sit!"

"I don't think he's going to sit, Carly," says my friend Montana from where she is swinging on the swing set. It's a little bit rusty, and it creaks like crazy.

"I know," I sigh and drop back into the grass. Too late, I think about dog poo and pee and wonder what I am lying in, but it's too hot to move. The grass is coolish and tickles my cheek. Montana swings over me. Her hair is fantastically long and black and swoops over my face as she passes, along with a little shower of rusty flakes from the chain.

Montana is from the Philippines. Her parents called her that because before she was born they decided to move to America, where there is more money than in the Philippines and it isn't so stifling hot all the time. They couldn't decide where to move to, so they threw a dart at the giant map of places to go and it landed on Montana. So for years and years and years they saved their money to move to Montana, and finally when they had enough gold pieces or whatever, they bought a ticket to America. Only it was a ticket to North America, not specifically America as in the United States, and they ended up here. In Victoria, B.C., Canada. At least, that's how Montana tells the story. I sort of wonder why they didn't change her name to Victoria, which everyone knows is not a bad name at all and can be shortened to Tory, which is a very good name. But they didn't. I like the name Montana. No one ever calls her Monty. She is a Montana, through and through — like mountains, and snow that is cool and white but so pretty that it hurts your eyes. And fresh, like melting glacier water.

I pick daisies while I lie on the grass. I am going to make Montana a daisy crown that she can wear on her head. She's my best friend in the whole world. She is even my best friend in the summer, now that school is finally over. Some friends are just school friends, and some friends stick for good. Me and Montana are the kind that stick. We're going to be best friends forever and always.

This afternoon, we are going to the pool. My mum and her mum signed us up for diving lessons, so we don't get bored and complain of nothing to do all summer long. I'm really excited but also just a teeny smidgen nervous. Mostly excited, but with a pinch of nervousness. What if she is excellent at diving and I just stand there and fall into the water on my belly, like I did at the cabin, and all the other kids laugh? What if something really awful happens, like that time at swimming lessons last year when someone threw up in the water and everyone had to get out of the pool? They fished it out with a net. The throw-up, that is. That could happen to me. I'm serious. Sometimes I get sick when I am nervous.

I lie in the grass and watch the sky get bluer and brighter and hotter, and inside, my stomach twists because I am excited and scared and looking forward to going to the pool and wishing I didn't have to go all at the same time.

"Let's practise gymnastics," Montana says.

So I jump up and start showing off, which is okay because even though I am way better at gymnastics than Montana is, she is better at piano and violin and tap dancing. It works out all right if everyone is good at something, don't you think?

I do cartwheels with my eyes wide open so I can see my house — well, it's really my New Dad's house, but also my house now — tipping over and over into the sky, getting all mixed up with the grass and the flowers and the swing set. I can even see the curtains in my room on the top floor and I can see my mum moving around in the kitchen. I keep going until I get too dizzy, and then I try to help Montana do a back flip, but she can't. She just drops backwards over my arm and gets stuck there in a really crazy back bend and her feet won't come up off the grass. It's actually very hilarious, and we laugh and roll around in the possibly-dog-pee-covered grass until Mum calls us to get ready to go.

I wear my new purple one-piece suit. I chose it very carefully. To be truthful, I made my mum buy it for me last week because my last year's one-piece didn't fit anymore. It was red, and I didn't really like it anyway. Still, I would rather have worn the red one than my favourite bikini. Every-one knows that bikinis are not cool to wear in the pool. They are only perfectly right if you are out-side, playing in the sprinkler or swimming in the sea. Only one-pieces are for inside.

There is one girl in the class wearing this little

yellow number, a bikini, of course, and me and Montana whisper a bit and giggle about the wrongness of her choice. Then I feel a little smidgen bad about that, so we tell her we were laughing at this boy with a fake tattoo who is also in the class, and she giggles, too. Her name is Samantha. Sam, for short, which is also a good name as names go. For instance, nothing rhymes with Sam except *ham* or *jam*, so she is not at much of a risk for getting a sudden sister with a rhyming name.

The teacher claps his hands to get our attention, so we turn to look at him and immediately get the giggles again because he is, like, movie-star good-looking, and we all must think it at the same time because we all start to smile, then laugh. Montana snorts when she laughs. Sometimes she isn't very dainty, I tell you.

His name is Jon. An okay name. He's so cute, he could be called Horace or Frank or something awful and it wouldn't much matter. We all try to calm down and listen closely so that he doesn't think we're laughing at him, which, I might add, we certainly are not.

He tells us to get in the water, so we do, which is perfect because then I can show off by doing an underwater handstand, even though I am not wearing goggles so the water stings my eyes. I love the smell of chlorine, the way it sticks into your hair and for the rest of the day people sniff the air and say, "It smells like someone's been swimming!" While I am goofing around, the class moves to the other side of the pool, and I come to the surface and I can't see them, and my heart beats a quick bit faster and I can tell I am in some kind of trouble.

Jon looks over at me and says, "If Carly has finished being silly, we can start the class now." I blush furiously, which is something that I am inclined to do because my skin is so pale and thin, like tracing paper. My veins and stuff make pictures inside my arms and on my legs. I can feel the beginning of the little plip-plops of madness, too, because he made me feel stupid. Quickly, I stare up at the window where the bright sunlight streams in, until the bubbles subside.

The first thing we do is watch Jon do a bunch of show-offy dives from the board. I guess it's fine for him to show off, but not for us. Talk about unfair. I don't like him much anymore, even though he probably will be a really famous movie star or maybe even do an ad for Coca-Cola one day. He does all these wild spinning, somersaulting, pointy-toed dives, then he swims back to us and says, "How many of you want to be able to do that?" and of course my hand flies into the air before I can stop it, and I start almost liking him again for wanting to show me how.

He picks Montana to do the demonstration of what we have to do. And that is jumping into the water with pointed toes. She does it beautifully, of course, maybe even a little bit better than me. Some of the boys can't seem to do it, and I can tell they won't last long. How hard is it to jump into the pool with pointed toes?

He chooses Sam for the next demo, which is crouching and arm swinging, just like I already tried on the rock. We do that for a long while and finally he touches me on the arm and says, "That looks good; why don't you try a real dive for the class?"

"Okay," I say, even though, to tell you the truth, I am a little bit skeptical. I certainly didn't notice the dive coming into me, and I am pretty sure I can't do it. But I agreed to try, so I'll try. He takes me down onto this little platform that is partway under the water, so the surface of the pool is half way between my knobby, scabby knee and my foot.

I stand there for a minute, or maybe more, and I wait for the dive to come.

And it does.

I don't know how or where it has been — hiding out in one of the pink and white cavities of my body somewhere, I guess — but here it is. I pull my arms back and over and my feet lift off and I cut into the water cleanly, like a knife through butter. At least, that's how it feels. When I surface a few metres away, the other kids are all staring at me, and I think maybe I've done something horribly wrong, or maybe when I dove in my bathing suit fell off or something like it does in dreams, but no. They are staring because I did it right.

Right then, at that exact second, I totally know that I want to do it again. And again and again and again.

And then the class is over.

I think Montana is a little bit jealous that it came so easily to me, so I tell her, in the car, our legs sticking to the dark vinyl seats, that I've been practising forever. Which isn't exactly true. I just knew when to stop and wait, that's all.

chapter 3

The boat catches the top of a wave and thuds down into the foam with a *thwack*. Montana reaches out and grabs the table.

"Ow!"

I giggle. "Sorry. It's a little bumpy."

Out the window, the waves are breaking with white frothy toothpaste tops that look like spit. Sorry, but they do. I think about telling that to Montana, but frankly, she looks a little pale. She's not used to being on boats like I am.

"Not much longer," I tell her. To be nice, I pass her Blue, who always sleeps on the boat. She sort of clutches on to him and pats his head and tells him it will be okay. Which it will, but I can tell it makes her feel better to look after him. His little wolfy ears are all soft and silky and she is patting them like mad. It makes me want to pat him, too, but she's my friend, so I won't. I mean, she needs him right now, what with the boat flipping and banging in the waves.

Marly and Shane are sitting up on the top with my New Dad. Apparently, it's less bumpy up there, and the fresh wind whipping their noses makes them not get sick. Mum had to go sit there, too, to make sure they don't go flying out of the boat when it hits a giant wave. Secretly, I don't think that would be such a bad thing, Marly bobbing around in the spit waves in her big orange life vest.

That was a mean thought. I am going to try very hard to unthink it, but you know how it is.

I am in a pretty fantastically happy mood this weekend because I was allowed to invite Montana to the cabin with us. We're going to practise our diving from the rock. After three weeks of lessons, I am, to tell you the real truth, a little worried: I think Montana might be a tiny teeny bit better at diving than me, even though it took her longer to catch on. I wanted to be better. I know, that's snotty and also show-offy of me, but I can't help it. That's just me.

Because the water is so messy, it takes us ages to get to the cabin, and by the time we get there it is not only past our bedtime, but also it is getting dark. The woods are just a tiny smidgen scary in the dark, because at the cabin there are no roads or streetlights or anything, just flashlights and the moon, and in the thick trees, let me tell you, the moon doesn't help a whole lot. Also, there are mosquitoes, which are very irritating and tend to buzz only in your ear, where it echoes around in your head until you are driven crazy. Montana is very brave, considering it is her first time here, and she is carrying her own backpack on her back without complaining, so I can't complain either. Even though I want to say something, because frankly the pack is pretty heavy, what with the books and whatnot I have brought. Mum and my New Dad carry the little kids as well as the food basket, so I guess I shouldn't whine. The dogs just galumph alongside us, without a care in the world. I think in my next life I would like to be a dog . . . or maybe a dolphin, or a bird. I haven't decided exactly which yet.

The next morning, we wake up to the sun streaming through the window and it is so hot upstairs in the loft where we sleep that, to tell you the truth, it is nearly impossible to breathe. I am sweating up some kind of storm, I can tell you that. Montana and I sneak down the ladder, trying not to wake up the kids (who are still snoring in their bunk bed), and the dogs, who sleep in the mud room at the back. Of course, the dogs wake up immediately and start whining and barking and yipping and yapping, so we quickly let them outside and they go running off into the woods. At the cabin, they can do that. It's not like they are going to disturb anyone, or get run over by a truck, or bark at the garbageman or anything.

"Have some breakfast," Mum calls sleepily from the bedroom.

I love the cabin, because we get to eat really sugary cereal that we can't eat at home. Don't ask me why. We fill our plastic bowls with Honey Smacks and take them outside on the front deck.

"Wow," says Montana, looking out at the sea.

I have to admit, it is pretty spectacularly beautiful, a big cedar deck that looks out over the Georgia Strait. About a hundred miles away, you can see Vancouver, so I point out to her the airport and Grouse Mountain, because they are about the only things I can identify. Oh, also Bowen Island, which is a distinct hill, and then a smaller hill. There is a ferry from there to Vancouver, so people can live in cabins and work in town. I think I'll do that when I grow up. I would like to have a purple cabin on an island, and a glamorous job in Vancouver. Purple on the inside, only. Obviously.

It's so quiet, you can hear the little *blip-blap* of the waves against the rocky beach. Like I said, there are no roads up here or anything, so there is no traffic. We're just sitting there, crunching our Honey Smacks and slurping the sweet milk, which is really the best part anyway, when we hear the dogs barking and freaking out. We get up to take a look, and suddenly we see these two deer go flying by, and behind them, waaaay back, the dogs go huffing and puffing and growling, Blue stumbling as he tries to keep up. Roo moves pretty fast for an old dog. Still, we can tell they don't have a chance of catching those deer. They are hoping against hope, as my mum would say. Not that that makes any sense. Still, the sight of it brings a smile to our faces.

Inside the cabin, we can hear the kids getting up and Mum and my New Dad getting them dressed. Those kids are really a pain. I roll my eyes at Montana. "Time to get out of here!" I tell her.

"We're going to the beach, Mum!" I stick my head in to tell her.

"By yourself?" She frowns, and I can tell she's worried.

"Motherrr . . . " I mean, it's not like I haven't been to the beach a million times before. What could possibly happen? We could fall and scrape our knees, maybe. But it's not like at home, where we have to worry about being kidnapped or about talking to strangers.

"All right," she sighs, like she's given up before the fight has even started. "But take the dogs with you and make sure you put on sunscreen; it's going to be hot today!"

"Yes, Mum . . . " I have to yell, because we are already halfway down the hill, running. Montana's hair flies out behind her like a sheet of glass. Mine just flip-flops limply against my back. Maybe I should shampoo more often and grow my hair long. Maybe I will one day when I have time.

The tide is way out. Like, I mean, way way way out. All the rocks are exposed, showing their shiny seaweed blankets to the sky. There is so much to do. I'm not kidding, it's perfect. First thing, I show Montana how to catch minnows in the tide pools using old ice-cream and margarine buckets. Some of the ponds are better than others. In the really big ones, there are too many places for the fish to hide. But there is one perfectly round pond that is about half a metre wide where you can just scoop your bucket around and catch dozens — maybe even hundreds — of minnows in one try. Minnows are very tiny fish. I think maybe they are baby salmon or something.

I don't really know. But they're cute, with big heads, and some of them have stripes. Some of them are just plain black.

We make them little aquariums in the buckets, putting in some pretty-coloured sand that is really just crushed shells: white from clams and oysters, blue from mussels. And then we add rocks and seaweed so that the little fish will feel more at home. Better than home, actually, like a hotel room instead of their same old boring house. They are probably quite excited, actually, by their new bucket rooms.

After that, we flip over some bigger rocks and I show Montana the eels. Frankly, I have never cared for eeling (which is what I call it when you catch eels), but she doesn't seem to be as grossed out by it as me. Eels are a type of particularly wet and slimy snake. They slither around under the rocks and flip-flop back and forth if you touch them. Montana says she has eaten eels before. Probably in the Philippines, I think to myself. It's no wonder they wanted to move to America. So of course I have to pretend it doesn't bother me, which it does, a tiny bit. Actually, a big bit. I mean, who would want to eat a big wriggling worm?

Pretty soon, it's so hot we can't stand it, and we

haven't even got to the part of the beach where there is the diving rock. We are still in plain view of the cabin. The dogs are flopped out in the shade, so we try to lure them into the water with sticks. I'm pretty excited because Blue follows Roo in this time, instead of standing on the beach like a dummy as he usually does. I sort of wish we could swim, too, but this particular spot is too rocky and sharp and wavy and cold. Not to mention slippery. One time, when I was younger, I slipped on these rocks and slid all the way down the slope and into the waves. I clonked my head really hard on the rock, and I can tell you, it hurt quite a lot. Sandstone might sound like something that could be soft, but it's not.

"We just have to go to the sandy beach," I tell Montana.

"Sure," she says.

But, of course, just then Marly and Shane come tumbling down the hill, followed by Mum and my New Dad, carrying a big basket full of food. Lunchtime! Which is perfect because I am splendidly hungry, my stomach just beginning to make the grumbling purring sound it makes right before I have to eat. We munch on our huge sandwiches with tomato and white bread and chicken and lettuce and glug back our root beer, and then it's time to go to the beach. Isn't it?

"Beach time," I say, jumping up off the log.

"Actually, we were thinking that today we should go for a walk in the woods," says my New Dad.

"Oooooh," I say. Already, I'm feeling kind of mad. I really really don't want to go on a stupid hike.

"What's the matter, Carly?" asks Mum.

"Nothing, Mum. I just . . . we just . . . well. We wanted to go to the sandy beach and dive off the rock." I'm trying not to cry, because I'm so mad, but I don't want Montana to see me being a baby.

"Ah, I see. Well, how about you do that tomorrow, and today we explore the woods?"

"Okay," says Montana. "That sounds like fun!"

So, I really can't argue, now, can I? If she is going to go along with it? I put on my pretend smile and poke Shane in the tummy and say, "Who's afraid of the deeeeeeep daaaaarrrrk wooooooodss?"

"Don't tease your brother," says Mum. And I can tell she's not kidding. It's easy to tell when she starts to get mad. She gets blotches on her cheeks. Really. Little round mad blotches. Like cherry tomatoes.

I mumble a bit of nothing under my breath so

that everyone knows that I am not really happy with this choice but I am going along with it because I am a good person. I kick a rock, too, actually. Probably, I broke my toe. It hurts quite a bit, like a bruise does when you press on it. But it's my own fault, so I don't say anything, I just limp along with them, while my New Dad leads us into the woods.

We spend the afternoon in the hot, dry forest. My New Dad keeps pointing out interesting stuff, like fungus growing on rotten trees, or stinging nettle, or a hole that a woodpecker made. Frankly, I am more than a little bored, until he starts telling us this story of some crazy guy who lived here a long time ago, like maybe twenty years, with a bunch of hippies. Anyway, his name was Brother XII, which actually is quite a strange name, I am sure you will agree. He was nuts, loony-toony, wacko, and he had a bunch of gold coins that he buried somewhere on the island. Or so my New Dad tells us. I mean, it might not be true. But still . . .

Montana and I look at each other and raise our eyebrows. Gold? Well, then, we could probably find it, couldn't we? We kind of dive into the bushes and start looking, like we're looking for Easter eggs. I don't know what we're thinking, maybe that it will just be lying there on the ground for anyone to find. We see a lot of moss and some deer poo and lots of prickly bushes, but no gold.

Finally, after wandering around in the salal bushes for an hour with the leaves scritching and scratching our legs, Mum and my New Dad say, "We should be getting back, the kids are tired."

And that's when me and Montana are free to really start our search seriously.

First thing we do, we look for the obvious places: under a big tree stump, in the middle of a clearing, by a strange-shaped rock. We don't find a thing! I didn't imagine it would be this difficult. Why would he hide it somewhere too tricky to be found? We put on our thinking caps, and think and think until our brain muscles start to hurt, then we decide, what the heck! We'll just start digging. I mean, clearly he wouldn't just leave it lying around for anyone to find. It must be buried.

So we do.

We dig and dig and dig through the soft dirt, getting dirtier and dirtier. And you know what? We don't find the gold, but we do find: one deer antler — which is quite a treasure even though it isn't gold — a tiny snail shell that looks like it is made of glass, and . . . a bee's nest!

So we end up running back to the cabin,

screaming and flapping to get away from those bees. We run really fast — my heart beating about a million beats a minute. We must look like those two deer that we saw this morning, just flying through the woods. I don't even feel the stings until we get back to the cabin. As it turns out, I got two stings, and Montana got three. She cries. I don't. I think maybe I am a little bit braver than she is, but that's okay. She's definitely prettier.

We didn't get any diving done this weekend at all. Frankly, that is too disappointing for words. We did build a neat fort in the woods, though, before we left on Sunday. We are going to use it as our clubhouse — no little kids allowed! I wish we could have gone to the beach, but it was cloudy and little spits of rain kept coming down, so Mum said we couldn't swim. I kind of like it when it rains at the cabin — it makes it smell so good. It just smells green, you know what I mean? And the fort we made was really cool. We built it from broken branches and driftwood that we dragged up from the beach. My New Dad even helped a little bit, cutting some logs for us. I made sure that he knew I would rather be swimming, though. I was still mad that he made us walk yesterday instead of doing what we wanted to do. I kind of think it's his fault that we got stung at all. It was his big idea.

Overnight, the bee stings made my leg swell up like a sausage, or something worse — a boiled frankfurter. I look gross. I wouldn't want to wear a bathing suit, anyway, if you know what I mean. And I'm sure you do.

Mum says Montana can come again, and we can even invite another friend. This probably saves her from having to listen to me teasing Marly and Shane — basically gets rid of me altogether. Hmmph. That's okay, though; I think I'll probably ask Sam, from diving class. Then, for sure, we'll practise our diving off the rock. Even if the weather isn't perfect. No more walks in the woods, I think to myself, even if there is gold.

chapter 4

You have have to know one thing — when you are standing on that springy diving board at the end of the pool (the white one), it is a lot higher up than you think it is when you are just walking by. I'm not kidding. The water is about twenty thousand metres down. I like the springy part, though, which is, of course, the problem. Jon is frowning at me.

"I think you've got the feel of the board now, Carly," he says. "Other people are waiting."

He's wrong. I don't have the feel yet. At least, I don't have the feel of how I can spring off the board into the air and then drop perfectly into the water. I don't. So I sort of crouch down and do a baby dive off the end. The board just kind of wiggles — it doesn't make that resounding, satisfying *wonka wonka* noise that it makes when someone really talented goes off. I love that sound.

Mine sounded more like a burp. I'm not kidding.

It was that bad.

As soon as I hit the water, I feel like crying. That was probably the worst dive in the history of the world. I can see my mum in the stands. She has Marly with her because her mum is at work and the sitter couldn't make it. Marly is clapping like mad, which makes me feel sadder because, really, it was an awfully lousy attempt.

What does she know? She's just a little kid.

Montana and Sam do much better, and watching them, I sort of feel the feeling that I should try it again so I sneak back into the lineup. Jon sort of wiggles his eyebrows at me as if to say, "What are you doing, little missy?" But I don't care.

This time, I don't even hesitate, I just jump. Way way up high, and then I find that I have a lot of time in the air to point my arms and toes, and down I go. The one tiny problem is that I go over a little too far and I come up facing the wrong way, with my face practically kissing the side of the pool under the board.

"Very nice," says Jon. Like he's surprised. Then he says, "See me after class." And I think, uh-oh, now I'm in trouble.

We spend the rest of the time out of the pool on

these little trampolines with stuff around our waist that lifts us way high up in the air. So we can get the feeling. I already have it, but I don't want to tell. Anyway, it's pretty much the most fun you can have, hanging from the ceiling in these rings. We use them for gymnastics, too, so I know some stuff. I do a couple of flips, to show off. I can't help it, there is something in my heart that kicks around and flaps and makes me do it. I swear. It's like a tremor.

I go to the change room with Sam and Montana and we goof around in the shower and it takes forever to dry our hair under those weird little dryers and I am halfway out the door to find Mum when I remember I was supposed to see Jon after class.

"Uh-oh!" I yell. I mean, I just shout it out right there in the hallway.

Everyone looks at me funny, so I kind of go, "Forgot something!" And I duck back through the change room and skirt around the shower so I don't get wet and go back to the pool. He's leaning over the guardrail talking to my mum. He's put on a sweatshirt that says Dolphin Diving Club. I guess he would have felt pretty stupid standing there half-naked. I mean, really.

Mum says, "Jon has an idea he'd like to talk to you about."

But I am already saying, "I'm sorry about barging into the line — I couldn't help it."

And Jon laughs and says, "That isn't what I wanted to talk about, but you're right, you shouldn't butt into the line and show off."

I look down and trace the pattern of the tile with the toe of my runner. It makes a squeaking noise which is overall quite interesting. I keep doing it until my mum says, "Stop it!" She says it in a loud, almost mean way. So I stop. I know when she means business.

I look up, and she says, a little more nicely, "Jon wanted to talk to you about joining the diving club and maybe taking some private lessons. If you're interested."

"Yes," says Jon, "I think you should. You certainly show some promise."

Show some promise! That's fantastic! I want to jump up and down and yell yippee! or something corny like that, but I try to be mature. I smile and say, "That sounds interesting."

"There's a local competition starting here in an hour," says Jon. "Maybe you want to hang out and watch and see if it's something that you want to try."

I'm, like, "Yes! Of course!" But I look at Mum and she frowns at her watch and looks at Marly. "I have to run Marly home first," she says. "But I guess we can fit it in and still make it to gymnastics."

"All right!"

"I want to watch the diving, too," says Marly in her whiny baby voice.

"No," I say. "You can't."

"Carly . . . "

"What, Mum?"

"Be nice to your sister," she sighs.

"Well, she can't stay, can she?" I'm kind of getting mad, again. I mean, this is about me, not about Marly. Mealy Marly. I just want one thing that is just for me.

So that's that. We take her home to her purple palace. "Princess Marly of the Purple Palace Apartments," I call her on the way up in the elevator. I mean it to be nice, but she kicks me in the shin anyway. Hard. I can feel a bruise starting. I don't do anything back. After all, she's just a little kid.

Back at the pool, I go sit in the stands with Mum. She buys me some nacho cheese chips with this gooey fake cheese all over them that is the best-tasting cheese in the world. Also, I am allowed to have some pop, which is pretty exciting because usually I get, instead, a lecture about cavities and tooth brushing. I'm pretty excited, so all this good food is probably a waste. I mean, I hardly notice that I'm eating anything. I could be eating a melted rubber tire for all I care.

The contest is for older kids, I guess; they all look like at least teenagers. The ones that are the most exciting are the high-board dives. Really. The board isn't springy, it's more a big concrete slab that, to tell you the truth, I didn't know was for diving off. They have to climb about a million stairs to get to the top. Boy, they must be pretty nervous, to be that high up and have all that time climbing to think about it. Some of them stand there facing the other way, hanging on with just their toes, then flip backwards and over and sideways and twist over and over before they hit the water. I hold my breath for the whole time they are in the air, that's how exciting it is. My knees feel a bit wobbly. I mean, they are only perched there on their toes like little tiny wingless birds, for goodness' sake.

I am so excited, I don't even eat my nachos, and the cheese goes all hard like glue. It's okay, though. I'm not even mad. Like I said, this is too fascinating to want to eat through. It's not like something boring that your mum makes you watch and buys you food to keep you quiet so she can enjoy herself. It's not like that at all.

The boy divers are much better than the girls. A couple of the girls splash in on their bellies and look sort of ashamed when they climb out. Actually, that is one thing I am going to have to work on if I am going to be a diver — I have a very difficult time climbing out of the pool without a ladder. These girls just put their arms on the tile and *flloooopp,* they push themselves up and out. I certainly have a lot of work ahead of me. My arms are more like wet noodles than anything. I would have thought I could do it naturally, what with all the gymnastics that I do. I would have thought it would be easier.

Next is the diving off the springboards, which are also much higher than the one I went off today. About ten or twenty times higher. These are neat, too, because of the extra height they get from the springiness. I try to watch carefully, to see how they do those somersaults and twists in the air, but frankly, the feeling isn't coming into me. I very much doubt that I could go down there right now and pull off one of those. I can somersault as well as the next person, but possibly not off the end of a springing, thwacking board.

"Wow," I say, when one boy flips up so high he practically hits his feet on the board higher up.

My mum smiles. I can tell she knows I'm

hooked. I'm like that — like a pit bull, my Real Dad used to say. I get an idea in my head and I just snap my jaw shut on it and don't let go until it's done.

I wish he was here. But I said I wasn't going to talk about that, didn't I? I'm just a kid, you can't expect me to talk about everything. Besides, my New Dad is pretty nice, sometimes. He's okay.

What more did you want me to say?

Okay. Listen up. This is it. This is really all I'm going to say.

My Real Dad died when I was still six. The part that bugs me a lot right now is that sometimes I have to struggle really hard to remember his face. Then, when I do, I can only imagine it one way — the way it is in the picture on the piano. Standing on the boat with the wind lifting his hair and blowing his shirt against his body.

That's all.

That's all I have to say about that.

I just think about him sometimes, is all I was trying to tell you. Sometimes, when something important happens, like today with the diving, I think about him a little more and I wish he was here instead of my mum. Which is mean, I know it is. I just can't help myself from wishing stuff, though, can I?

chapter 5

It's flat calm when we take off on Friday to go to the cabin, and it's pretty sunny so I think for sure we'll be able to do some swimming. Even better, Marly and Shane are spending the weekend with their mum and her new boyfriend. They went camping in a trailer, or something. Whoop-de-doo. That won't be nearly as much fun as the cabin. I don't care, though. I'm excited because it's just me and Sam and Montana, and Mum and my New Dad, of course.

The water is glassy smooth, like a mirror. You can see the reflection of the boat and of the sky, which is perfect blue and hot. The sun is a shiny disk of heat, like a really hot penny.

Mum has slathered sunscreen goop all over all of our faces because she says we'll burn like eggs on the sidewalk if she doesn't. Also, we all have to wear hats. We sit in the back in a little row, and we can't talk much because of the roaring scream of the engine. The dogs sit way up at the front; they can't get far enough away from that sound. I think it hurts their ears. Anyhow, they always usually sleep the whole trip.

I look over at Montana and Sam in their hats and sunglasses and my heart does this *p-tink, p-tink* with excitement. It's going to be a perfect weekend. I can tell already. Montana grins at me and yells something about our fort, which I can't really hear because, like I said, it's pretty noisy. And then Sam swings her arms like a dive, and I get more excited. Sam joined the diving club with me, but Montana didn't. She decided to take ballet instead. Sam isn't as good at the gymnastics part of diving as me, but whooooo-eeeee, she is as brave as anyone.

The first time we went off the higher springboard, I got a little bit nervous. Okay, a lot nervous. More like terrified. I stood there for, like, an hour, before I could jump off. Sam, though, she just flung herself into the air, no worries. Even after her bikini top flew off in the pool, she was totally unfazed. I mean, I would have been embarrassed and blushing to beat the band. She really does need to get a better swimsuit. Jon said that we could buy some Dolphin Diving Club suits so that at the big meet in the fall, we will look professional. I guess it doesn't matter whether we look professional or not at the other meets. There won't be anyone really important to impress until the last one; then there will be people from out of town, not just people from around here. I'm kind of nervous about it, to tell you the truth.

I don't want to talk about that now. It makes my knees wiggle with fright. The hardest dive that I am going to do is super-complicated. It's part of a somersault, and part of a twist, and it starts facing backwards. I know there are people who do, like, three somersaults and two twists in one dive, but I'm not that good. And I am just getting used to that — facing backwards. It still doesn't feel quite right.

I'm going to practise this weekend. Until I get the feeling for it.

That's the secret to everything that grown-ups never tell kids. The secret is just to wait until you get the feel. The rest is easy.

The boat skims along the water. My New Dad steers so that we kick up a really wild wake, which is cool. One day, he promised, we'll get a water ski, and then we can learn to do that behind the boat. I close my eyes and imagine myself waterskiing all the way up to the cabin. That would be really something, wouldn't it?

Swoosh, swoosh, swoosh over all that wake. I think I could probably do it the whole way, even if it is just over an hour. My arms are pretty strong now because I have been practising getting out of the pool with no ladder. I can do it now, no problem. Easy breezy.

When we land, it's still light. Which is much better than the last time Montana was here when we had to go through the woods in the dark. This time, because it is light, Mum says we can set up the tent and sleep outside tonight! Frankly, I am a little worried about it because once I saw something in the woods that might have been a cougar. I'm not saying it was. My Real Dad always said there were no cougars on the island. However, it was an awfully large-looking, golden-coloured cat. I imagine us all sleeping in the tent, and the cougar saying, "Hmmm, that looks like a nice comfy place to spend the night." He would come right inside, using the zipper, and see us all sleeping there, and maybe he would say, "My, what a delicious-looking pile of little girls!" You can imagine what would happen next. Really.

"I love sleeping in tents," yells Sam. So I can't say I don't want to now, can I?

I sneak a look at Montana, but she looks happy, too, so right away we set about finding a place to put it, or *pitch* it, I should say. That's what you do. You pitch a tent.

We settle on a mossy patch that is within shouting distance of Mum and my New Dad's bedroom window. I can feel myself relax a bit inside. It's much too close to the cabin for a cougar to be interested, I am sure. Also, Mum says that Blue can sleep in the tent with us, for protection. I don't know how much help he would be in an emergency, but what the heck. He is getting bigger, less loose and floppy than he was before. Maybe he would look scary to a cougar. I don't know. At least if he started barking, we might have time to run into the cabin, or at least up a tree to escape. There is a perfect tree right near the tent. It is a sloped kind of arbutus tree that you can walk up because of the way it bends. Of course, maybe cougars can climb. That would be a fine mess. We would have to climb all the way to the top and jump onto the roof of the cabin, which is really steep so we would have to hold on tight. I don't even know if we could jump that far. This might not be a good idea. I want to mention the cougar to the others, but then I think another thought: probably, I shouldn't scare them. They are my guests, after all. I should be brave and pretend there is no problem. That's what my mum would do, I'm sure. Also, seeing as I am ten now, I am too grown-up to worry about things like cougars. I'm not a baby anymore.

The sleeping bags smell funny, like old dust. And the air in the tent smells of plastic and grass that has gone to seed. We leave the window open a crack to let the fresh air in to cool us. It's not particularly cool, I can tell you that. Already we have thrown off the heavy sleeping bags. The tent is like a microwave. If we were microwave popcorn, I tell you, we'd be popping. *Pop, pop, pop.*

We stay up forever, talking and talking. That's the best part about having best friends, you can tell them anything. I tell them I am thinking of giving up gymnastics and focusing just on diving. I want to be in the Olympics, I tell them. Like when I am older, maybe sixteen or seventeen.

Montana says she wants to be either a doctor, like her mum, or a movie star, or perhaps someone who works with poor children or children who have lost their arms and legs in terrible farm-equipment accidents or the like. She once knew someone who knew someone that this happened to. I don't want to mention that there may not be that many children in that situation in Victoria.

Maybe in the Philippines. I don't know. I've never been there.

Sam wants to be an astronaut. She has this wild idea of living in a bubble on another planet. A bubble with a pool, she adds, so she can dive in space. She is thinking that maybe Venus would be a good planet, because it has the best name. Or Saturn, due to the rings. Her dad told her that in her lifetime there would probably be places to visit on the other planets, so she figures she'll have a home there, no problem. I don't say anything, but I think that's kind of silly. Her dad should probably know better.

"Good night, girls," Mum calls from the deck. "Lights-out time!"

We turn off the little battery lamps and lie in the dark. Pretty soon, almost right away, our eyes adjust and we can see perfectly well.

"When I grow up, I want to marry Jon," whispers Sam. This is the kind of secret that can only be told in the dark. There is quiet for a couple of minutes, then I say, "Me, too," even though I am not sure this is true. I just didn't want her to feel like she was the only one.

Montana doesn't say anything. I can hear her breathing kind of thicker than she was before, so I know she is asleep. Just listening to her breathing and Blue snoring puts me right to sleep. If Sam said anything else, I sure didn't hear it.

We sleep right through until morning, and when we wake up it is approximately five thousand degrees in the tent.

"Aaaaaarrrgghhhh," we scream. Blue is panting like crazy, like a maniac. We scramble out of the tent and run barefoot to the outhouse, and into the cabin for our sugar cereal.

Pack our beach bags.

Change into our suits.

Grab the Frisbees for the dogs.

Gulp down some water.

"We're going to the beach," I yell to Mum.

"Okay," she says sleepily. "We'll be down in a little while." Luckily, she is still almost asleep and so doesn't give us a three-hour lecture about being careful and wearing sunscreen.

We run all the way through the woods. The dogs are galumphing along beside us, crashing through the bushy parts of the trail looking for deer and squirrels and raccoons and whatnot. By the time we get there we are so hot, we just want to plunge into the ice-cold water, but . . .

Bad news.

The tide is way out. So far out that the whole

sandy bay is turned into a giant sandy beach. The water is a million miles away. The diving rock sticks up in the middle of the sand like a statue.

"I don't think we should dive from that rock," says Sam.

"No," I say. "Not yet."

But . . .

There are lots of really super things to do when the tide is way way out, let me tell you.

First of all, the most fun thing to do is to build a giant sandcastle. If you have lots of time, you can build one that is just huge, and then, when the tide comes in, you stand on it, and you don't get wet. It's like your own island. Sometimes I would have contests with my Real Dad, like who could build the biggest castle, and who got wet first. I haven't played that with anyone for a long time, and I kind of want to do it now. I tell the girls, and they agree, so we set to work piling up sand. It is hot work, I'm not kidding. We carry tons and tons of sand into the middle of the bay and build up and up and up, three lumps of sand. That way, we all have our own island to stand on, and we can play the game.

The sand is grey and wet and gritty and sticks to your skin until you are so itchy, you can hardly stand it, but we keep building. Every once in a

while, one of the dogs comes over and starts digging next to us, but it's really too hot for them. They
give up quickly. One thing that happens while we
work is that Roo gets hold of a starfish and eats off
a couple of legs. It's pretty disgusting, as I am sure
you can imagine. We throw it deep into the sea, and
throw its two legs out after it. Someone told me
once that starfish regrow their legs, like earth-
worms will regrow if you accidentally chop them in
half with a trowel. I hope that Roo made three
starfish out of one, but I have a feeling it will just
be one sorry starfish with two smaller legs.

Also, while we are digging, we find a sort of
gross sand centipede thing that looks like a worm
but bigger. I have never seen one before. I am worried that maybe it bites. Who ever heard of a sand
worm? It sounds like something from outer space.
Possibly this is a very dangerous worm. I swallow
down the big bubble of fear that bumps around in
my throat and throw the worm as far as I can.
Wait. This is the gross part — I don't throw it far
enough and Roo goes running over like mad and
eats the worm-thing. I'm not kidding. Sam and
Montana are killing themselves laughing. It's not
their dog, though. I hope Roo doesn't get sick.
Starfish and sand worm sound pretty bad to
me. I pretend to laugh, too, so they don't think I'm

wimpy, but really. Think about it.

The tide is sweeping in now; it trickles over the hot sand and creeps towards us really quickly. We start squealing and jumping and build our castles as high as humanly possible before we climb on top. Roo and Blue run back to shore, because that water comes in really, really fast. *Whooosh.* It's pretty shallow — I don't want you to think we were in grave or immortal danger or anything. It's only a little bit deep.

Gradually, it starts to make our sandcastles sink and sink. Sam's crumbles first and she is standing knee-deep in cold water, shrieking like a banshee. Then mine sort of sighs and dissolves and I'm right there with her. Montana is still perched on hers, like the queen of the castle. We can't have that! We start splashing her and finally, finally, hers is swallowed by the tide.

Mum and my New Dad show up with lunch, so we go sit on the logs and throw sticks for the dogs and eat our most delicious pizza that Mum made in the propane stove. It's amazing how much like home a cabin can be — you could probably survive here for at least a year or so without having to go to the store as long as you planted a garden and brought lots of canned food. Sometimes I think about doing that, about just staying here and living off the land. I can imagine myself waving goodbye to Mum and my New Dad, and watching the boat disappear in the distance. Maybe it would be lonely, after all.

After lunch, we lie around on the rock, sleepy like the seals on the reef. It's really very pleasant in the sun.

Finally,

after we wait almost all day,

it's deep enough to dive off the rock.

It's a little different than the springboard at the pool, that's for sure. But the water is nice and deep and clean today. There is not a lot of junk floating in it like that other time when we were here before the summer holidays had started. Mum says that has to do with the tides. Whatever. We all line up in a row and do regular dives off the rock, climbing in and out.

After a while, though, we decide to get fancy.

We do somersaults into the water.

We do backwards dives.

We do jumping dives and try to touch our toes in the middle.

It's getting late, so it's almost time to go. The water has that black-glass shadow look, and Sam's lips are turning a little blue. We don't want to stop, though. We're having too much fun.

We just have to do it one more time.

Do you ever regret doing something one more time, when you know you should stop?

This is what happens:

We all line up to do our best dives. One, two, three. I see the sky flip over my head as I go into the water. I pop up on the surface and see Sam, and we start swimming to the beach. But where is Montana? Right away, I feel that fast-sinking, scared feeling in my stomach.

"Mum! Dad!" I call, but my voice is all scratchy and weak. I can tell that something is very wrong. It's like in a bad dream when you try to shout, and you can't.

"What's the matter?" asks Sam. She's swimming on her back, looking at me.

"Montana," I mouth.

She doesn't come up.

"Mr. FITZ!" Sam screams. She certainly has a good screaming voice, which I never knew before. It's a good thing, because I'm just kind of gasping, not making any sound. The water looks blacker and smoother than ever before, and there is just me and Sam bobbing there, her screaming, and me just sputtering.

He is there in a flash. I guess he can tell very quickly what happened. He dives into the water and he disappears into the black for what feels like a long time. Then, finally, he pulls Montana up. Her eyes are wide open and her lips are making little fish movements. The really bad part is that her arms and legs are all floppy. He drags her in to the beach and puts her down and she just lies there looking up at the sky, her mouth moving.

Luckily, Mum brought the cell phone and is calling the Coast Guard quick as can be.

I kneel down on the sand beside Montana and hold her hand and start singing this song we made up at school. It's about boys and flowers and clouds and fields and big hairy warts. It's sort of a nonsense song, which I'm sure you figured out all on your own. Blue comes over and presses his face against Montana's tummy. She just looks at him, and says in a really strange whispery voice, "I can't feel that. I can't feel that."

I'm really scared. I can tell you that. I'm shaking like crazy.

The hovercraft is there in a flash. It's this huge boat on wild big balloon things and it just whips right up onto the beach. Which would be really something to see if it wasn't so scary. It comes right over the rocks like they are nothing. Like they are invisible dust. There are a bunch of men on the boat, and they gently push me out of the way and then strap Montana onto a board and load her into the boat.

Mum goes with her.

That's what happens. They just take her and then they are gone, leaving us standing there in the sand, shivering because we are still all wet and the sun is thinking about sinking low and melting the sky into orange and pink.

It's that late.

chapter 6

For one thing, I hate the smell of hospitals. I never knew that before, but I know right away as soon as I step in the door, that half the reason people are sick is because of the smell. It's like antiseptic and floor wash and something worse, something I don't even want to think about. I haven't seen Montana for three whole weeks. I mean, it's August already. That's a long time to go without seeing your best friend. It's sort of turning bad outside, less like summer and more like back-to-school time, when it tends to rain and be cloudy more than usual. Today I am wearing a long-sleeved shirt, that's how not-nice it is.

My shoes squeak against the floor, which reminds me of happier times — how the same sound is made by runners on a wet pool deck. The hospital is full of people who look busy. Also, there are old people sleeping on stretchers in the hallway, which I think is a little bit creepy. I imagine I'll be having some bad dreams regarding this. I'm not sure how they will be, but already I can feel my brain turning these halls into something scary.

We take the blue elevator up to the children's ward. There are teddy bears and kids' drawings stuck on the bulletin board in there, which feels friendly and maybe okay, or even a little bit babyish. But still better than the rest of this place, that's for sure. The nurse comes out right away and greets us, like she is the Avon lady or something. She is smiling and friendly, and right away I think, boy, she should sell makeup. I'd buy a lipstick from her, definitely. She has a shiny face that makes you want to look better.

Anyway, she tells me that Montana looks a little different, but she's still the same, so I shouldn't act different around her. They have put a steel rod in her spine, I'm told, but she is lucky because she can move her arms and legs. I guess she broke her back. I don't know why they didn't put it back together with something a little more flexible than a steel rod, but I guess that's why I'm a kid, not a doctor. I sort of wonder if maybe we'll be able to put magnets on her back and they'll stay there, which would be quite interesting. I also know from the nurse's face that this is not the right time to ask. Maybe I'll ask Montana. She's probably already found out about stuff like that.

Actually, I think I might feel a little bit jealous already. I'll never have a steel rod in my back. It sounds sort of neat. Like getting crutches or a cast on your arm. Sort of dangerous, but also cool.

I go into the room first, and her mum is there, and she comes over and gives me a hug and says that she is going to go down to the cafeteria to get a sandwich and maybe a piece of pie. I'd like a piece of pie myself, but I don't say anything. How often do I get a piece of pie? When I grow up, I am going to go for a piece of pie all the time. I'll say to my kids, "Wait here, Mummy's going to have some pie in a restaurant." Oh, goodness. Instead, I go over to the big bed where Montana is lying. She does look different. She looks so different that I feel these big hot tears directly behind my eyes, trying to come out. I have to blink really hard. For one thing, her long beautiful hair has been cut off. Now her head is all shaggy, like a boy's. Also, she is skinnier, and not in a good way. In more of a starving-crow way.

"Hi," I say quietly. I feel like I need to talk quietly in here like you would in a library. First thing

I want to do is ask her about her hair, but I don't want to make her feel any worse.

"Carly!" Her eyes fly wide open. "I'm so glad you're here! It is so boring in here, I can't stand it! Tell me everything."

"Everything? Like what?" I can tell my voice sounds funny, but it is just adjusting to this new Montana.

"Everything. About what you've been doing."

Suddenly, I don't want to tell her, because frankly, I feel a little bit bad about playing with Sam and diving and gymnastics and taking Blue to obedience school. Ordinarily these would have been things Montana would have been doing, too.

"Not much," I say. "It's been pretty boring without you."

"Really?" She sounds so hopeful. I was right to not tell the whole truth, I think. I don't want to make her feel worse, after all.

"Yeah," I elaborate. "I've just done a lot of sitting around. Reading. You know. I haven't even bought any back-to-school clothes."

Now that is an out-and-out lie, because just yesterday Mum bought me a bunch of cool stuff at the Gap which I had been wanting quite badly. I just love their new ads on TV. My New Dad says I'm just being sucked in to all the media brainwashing. But I don't care. The clothes look really good. Anyway, just at that moment, Mum comes in and says, "Did you tell Montana about your shopping spree?"

And I sit there and say, "Gee, Mum, I forgot about it! I don't know where my head is." I kind of roll my eyes, like I can't believe how stupid I was to forget. And I tell Montana all the stuff I got. It turns out okay, though. She looks really happy, almost as if she got all this stuff, too.

This is what I got: a red shirt and a blue shirt and two pairs of jeans and a baggy pair of khaki pants and a sweater and a white shirt. The sweater is very cute. It is pale blue and there is a butterfly embroidered on the front. I don't tell Montana about that because I don't want her to feel sad that she is here and not out buying new soft clothes with butterflies.

I think she feels sad enough as it is.

I forget to ask her about the magnets, even though that was very important when I came in. I forget, what with all the wires and beeping and the smallness of Montana. It looks like some of the water has been pulled out of her and her skin is a little too big. It's so weird. I can't quite get my thoughts straight on the subject of how she looks. It's very distracting.

Then, before I can ask her, she says, "They cut all my hair off because they couldn't move me around to wash it and stuff. It was just a mess and it smelled bad and was all in knots. So I told them to cut it off, and they did."

"Wow," I say. Because, to tell you the truth, I'm really impressed. I wouldn't be cutting off my hair for all the tea in China, I'm sure. And my hair is nowhere near as nice as hers was, that's for certain.

I sit there for a long time, and we don't say much, until I think maybe she is asleep and I get ready to tiptoe out of the room so I don't wake her up. She looks very pretty and fragile when she is sleeping, like a china doll.

But I guess my shoes must make a noise, because she wakes up and she calls me back to the bed and says, "It wasn't your fault, you know. I just dove too deep and hit that big sunken log. I just want you to know that I don't blame you."

I hug her very carefully, and think about her steel-rod back and kiss her cheek and say, "I know you don't."

But the funny thing is, until she suggested it, it didn't occur to me that I should feel bad. And now I do.

Boy oh boy. It must be my fault or why would

she say that? Why didn't I think of that right away? I am very worried that maybe I am not a good person. A good person would have noticed right away and said something like, "I'm really sorry I invited you to the cabin and you dove off the rock into a big sunken log and broke your back."

What kind of friend am I?

Not a very good one, I am sure you are saying. Don't worry. I'm sure I agree with you. Yes, sir. I sure do.

Diving practice is going really badly, because I keep trying to dive with my back super metal-rod-straight, to see what it would be like. I have belly-flopped about a hundred times, and finally Jon comes over and says, "I think that's enough pool work for you today." Which is good because my skin is on fire. I peek down the front of my suit to make sure, and it looks like my stomach has some kind of severe and possibly fatal sunburn. Also, it feels like it is tingling and numb. I do it one more time, though. I can't help it.

It hurts.

Jon calls out, "Enough, Carly! I mean it!"

Mum told him about the accident, and ever since then he has treated me differently. More gently, or something. I don't think I like it. I say,

"I am just fine, and I want to work on this dive." I say it as snootily as I can. I feel mad — I am not sure why.

"No," he says, "I think you should do some work in the gym."

So I sigh, like I've really had enough, and stomp off to the change room to put on my dry stuff. I do feel a little better in the gym, I have to admit. There is a coach for the inside stuff named Cassie, and she is really sweet. She used to be a ballerina. She helps me with my trampoline work, and with my legs and stuff. I work really, really hard. I work so hard that my hair gets wet from sweat. I work until I can hardly picture Montana in that giant bed surrounded by those alien beeping machines. I can hardly remember what she said.

We have a whole bunch of meets this summer. Most of them are just fake meets, if you ask me, because the only people who get to go are the people already *in* the Dolphin Diving Club. I mean, what's the point of competing against the same old people that you dive with every day? It's kind of dumb. But later, there are some bigger competitions, where people come from all over the island, and even later still there is a really big-deal meet for the whole province. That's the one I care about.

Think about it. It's really the only one that counts.

The schedule for the big-deal meet is posted by the time I leave. I look for my name, and it isn't there, and for a second I get scared, like maybe I am not allowed to dive this time because of what I did to Montana. Then I realize I'm looking at the wrong list.

Phew!

There I am. October 9, 9:00. That's only two months away. I am in only one event, but it is my favourite, springboard. Yippee! Sam is in two, but she is doing a high dive and I'm not. To be honest, the high platform scares the bejeebies out of me. I love the springboard, though. I can't wait. But at the same time, I think, maybe I shouldn't be doing this. Maybe I should quit before I get hurt. Maybe I should quit because I did a bad thing and I don't deserve to be having so much fun. I don't want to think that way, but I can't stop. It's like when you get a song stuck in your head and you keep singing it over and over and over again.

I feel funny inside. Like that frozen Jell-O stuff that Mum makes, cold and pink and wiggly. Like I am afraid of something, but I don't know what.

At dinner, Marly spits her spaghetti out her nose while she is laughing. Honestly, I don't think I was ever that weird. Sam is staying with us this week, because her parents are away visiting her grandma and she didn't want to go. After dinner we'd planned to take the dogs down to the park, but Mum says we have to take Marly and Shane, too. I roll my eyes. For goodness' sake. We are like free babysitters. Sam seems to really like Marly. Huh! She says, "Great! We can play on the swings!"

My New Dad looks over and says, "You be careful."

And that brings back the accident like a speeding bullet that lands in the middle of the table. I sit there until my madness bursts out and I say, "If you can't trust us with the kids, maybe they shouldn't come with us."

I storm out of the house and try to slam the door, which doesn't work because it is on springs. I grab Roo, because Blue is nowhere in sight, and go running down the street. I like running. I like the bumpy, hot pavement smashing into my feet and the smell of cut grass and the fact that my heart beats so loud I can hardly hear my thoughts.

The park isn't any fun without Sam. I regret it right away. I sit on the swing by myself and hold my back really straight and think about Montana and the daisy chain I made her and how she was going to grow up to be a movie star or at least a doctor if she wasn't pretty enough for film.

I guess that can't happen now. I've never heard of a movie star with a rod in her back. Maybe she could still be a doctor. I hope so.

I swing back and stare up at the sun until I see little dots. Then I keep staring until the little dots turn into big blotches, and I close my eyes and watch the patterns on the back of my eyelids. I stay at the park until the clouds start to roll their big, heavy, grey rainy-ness overhead. The first rolling drums of thunder send Roo running home without even a look over her shoulder.

"Thanks a lot," I tell her. It doesn't matter. She's already gone.

I go home, too. It rains on me, the whole way. Hard little pellets of dryish rain that sting my skin. I sort of feel like crying, but I don't. Instead I just breathe in the smell of wet pavement and think about all the diving meets coming up, and the big meet in October, and I think about how Sam is almost like my best friend now, too. And I think about going back to school without Montana.

I'm going to save her a seat, though. I don't want to sit next to anyone else, even if she does look a bit funny. She is still my Montana, after all.

She's still my best friend. Sam's my almost-best friend, but Montana still has the top spot, as far as I'm concerned. I don't care about her hair and the steel rod and stuff. I don't care about any of that. Really. I don't.

chapter 7

"No, Shane, like this." I scoop the bucket around the minnow pool and show him the tiny fish.

"Uh-uh," he says, grabbing it from me and spilling the poor little guys all over the rock.

"Great," I yell. "Now they're going to die."

I try really hard to pick them all up from where they are flip-flopping all over the place, but some of them get stuck between barnacles or slip into the crack in the rocks. I pour a bucket of water over them. I'll just have to sit here and pour water over them until the tide comes back in. That should take forever. I imagine that I'll be here all night, still sitting here on this patch of brown and purple seaweed under the stars with mosquitoes buzzing in my ears. I'll be starving. What am I thinking? I can't save these fish.

I can't save anyone.

"You killed them," I hiss at Shane. And, of

course, he bursts into tears and wobbles over to his dad, who is watching from a pile of logs. He practically falls on his head about ten times, which makes him cry harder. Well. He really shouldn't be stepping on the wet green seaweed. Everyone knows the green stuff is slippery when it's wet. I know he's just a baby, but he has been told about a thousand times. Probably more than that. If there is one way that my New Dad is like my Real Dad it is in their love for saying, "Don't slip on the green stuff!"

Huh. You'd think we would all have that figured out by now, wouldn't you?

"What you doing, Carly?" I look up and there is Mealy Marly staring at me with her big googly eyes.

"Nothing, Marly," I sigh. I sigh twice, actually, for good measure. So she'll know for sure that I'm just not interested in talking to her right now.

"What that water?" she asks, crouching down in that way that little kids have. She's staring at the flip-flopping minnows, which are flip-flopping quite a bit less than before, I might add.

"Go away," I tell her, as nicely as possible under the circumstances.

"Carly, you tell me what you doing. I tell Dad."

"Okay, fine. If you have to know everything, Miss Busybody Bum, I'm trying to save these little fish from dying. Your brother killed them," I say. I glare at her with my best evil eyes.

"Why?"

"I don't know, ask him."

"I help?" Honestly, that kid doesn't give up. She's kind of grinning at me, too, like we're old friends. Which we certainly are not.

"No, go away," I tell her. "I mean it. Get lost."

Ever since the accident, I haven't had much patience with the kids. Okay, I didn't have much patience with them before. But before, I didn't always feel like crying all the time. The fish have all stopped flopping and sort of just lie there, and I know that they are dead. Great. Big, baby tears escape from my eyes, stinging, and I turn and run up the hill towards the cabin. It's slippery, and I almost fall all the way to the top. It's been raining like mad. Like crazy. The sandstone and moss are all slimy with rain. But who cares? I have to run — who needs to let a kid see you crying?

This is our last weekend at the cabin. School goes back on Monday. Montana missed the whole summer, just because I asked her to come here with me. If I hadn't asked her . . . well. As you can imagine, everything would be different. Or the same, is what I mean. Everything would have stayed the same as it was before.

It would have been perfect.

Blue comes snuffling around my feet as I slip and slide up the trail towards the cabin. He's grown like a weed this summer, I can tell you that. He's about half the size of Roo now, and Roo is pretty big. Giant, really. Anyway, Blue is bigger but doesn't seem any more mature; he still trips over his feet and chases butterflies and stuff. I wish I was a puppy. Blue doesn't worry about anything. He's still the same as he always was. I glare at him then. I mean, the rest of us have had to change a lot. I haven't even been swimming at the sandy beach since the accident. I don't really think I will ever go there again.

On the deck out front of the cabin, I have put up a tent made out of sheets and towels. Mum lent me an old air mattress, which I have filled up with all of my own air, which is quite interesting if you think about it. This green plastic mattress has hundreds — or maybe even thousands — of my very own breaths trapped inside. So I have the mattress in my tent and some books and paper. I am making a map of the island and marking all the likely spots for Brother XII's treasure to be hidden. Maybe if I find it I can hire a really good doctor to patch Montana's back together again.

Money can buy almost anything, I know it can. I heard my New Dad say that once. Gold is a particularly excellent kind of money because it looks like coins but is worth a lot more. I imagine that Brother XII's treasure is a big chest of gold coins. I promise you, I will find it. Frankly, I can't imagine why no one has found it yet. It's money! It's free for the taking for anyone who finds it!

Inside my tent, it is shady and cool and dry and a nice bit private. The kids aren't allowed to talk to me when I am in here. Sometimes, I lie back on the mattress and close my eyes and imagine different things. For example, I imagine myself doing a perfect armstand with three somersaults and a bunch of twists off the high platform. Or I picture myself doing the dives I am actually going to do at the big meet in October. We have already decided. These are: some basic, boring easy dives in pike and tuck; forward somersault in pike position; back somersault in tuck position; and, the hardest of all, back somersault with a half-twist. That one has a 1.7 degree of difficulty. I'm not very good at that one yet, and I have to go in for extra practicing every week until the competition. I'm not going to do it at any of the earlier meets, because to tell you the truth, I can't quite do it at all. Well, I can do it on the trampoline with that thing around my waist, no problem. But when it comes to the actual pool? Forget it. I can't feel it. I told you before, that's all that matters. Feeling it filling you up and telling your arms and feet which way to go.

So that's what I am doing — I am imagining myself doing that one perfectly.

One thing — did I tell you this? — one thing that I love about diving is that last second when you lift off from the board and you have to decide in your mind which dive you are going to do, how you are going to tuck your head in, or twist your hips or your shoulders. It's sort of like flying gymnastics. There is something about that last tiny minute. Anything could happen. You could go any way you want, and no one knows what you are going to do. Unless you've told them, of course. Unless it's written down there beside your name on the entry form. Jon's probably wishing he hadn't written down "back somersault with half-twist" beside my name, I can tell you that. He was probably thinking that I'm a lot more talented than I actually am.

I wish Montana hadn't gotten hurt while she was diving. It's taking the shine off, a bit. Like, it used to be this thing I really loved, but now part of me squinches up inside when I think about it, and right away I start thinking about the steel rod in her back. I hope they built some little hinges into it. They must have done something so at least she can bend over. How will she tie her shoes? I hope they thought of that. I close my eyes and imagine Montana doing all the stuff we used to do, and then I do have this tiny comforting idea about Montana — remember I said she was really good at piano? Well, she can still do that, can't she?

I keep my eyes closed and I picture her at the piano with her back nice and straight and her hair glossy and long again, and I think maybe it will work out after all. You need good posture to play the piano well. I don't play anymore, but when I did, my teacher made me put a book on my head and walk across the room. She said I slouched at the keyboard and my posture was crummy. Well. Also, she smelled of tea and cookies. If she didn't like what I was playing, she blinked like crazy. You can imagine why I quit. Really, she was very annoying.

Besides, I like doing stuff with my body better than music. I've been so busy with diving and all those weekends at the cabin, that I haven't been to gymnastics for a month. But I'll go back when school goes back. Back to the parallel bars that bruise my hips.

To tell you God's honest truth, I am also thinking about school a little bit. Actually, quite a lot. I mean, Montana won't be there, right? And Sam goes to some other school on the other side of town. So I'll sort of be all by myself. It's not that I don't know anyone else. It's just that I don't know them really well. And I think, maybe, that they will all have heard about Montana and they'll ask me questions, and what happens if I get upset and have to run out of the room? What happens then?

I hear a little *scribble-scrabble* noise, so I poke my head out of my blanket tent, and wouldn't you know it — a raccoon is in the dog dish, eating the dog food. It's completely adorable. He has these little mini hands, and he is scooping out pieces of food and rinsing them in the water dish. I giggle, because it's so sweet, but he hears me. He sits right up on his back legs and looks at me as if to say, "Who are you? What do you want?" Then he grabs another handful of food and takes off into the bush.

The dogs must have gone back down the hill with Mum. They wouldn't stand for a raccoon in their dinner. No, sir. They would be barking up a storm, chasing the poor little guy up the very tallest tree. I remember once Roo kept a raccoon up a tree all night. He had to sleep up there, with Roo sitting at the bottom growling if that raccoon so much as moved a muscle. Once, Blue cornered one down on the beach against a big rock when he was too little to know better. That raccoon was fighting mad, I can tell you that. He just reached out and swiped his claw across Blue's nose. Blue bled like a maniac. He was so surprised he just yelped and sat down, and the raccoon ran away. He still chases them, though. I don't know why. It's like the slippery green stuff on the rock. How hard is it to learn that kind of lesson? Really. Sometimes I think Blue isn't even as smart as Shane, and that's saying something.

I crawl back into the tent and close my eyes. The sun is coming out from behind the rain clouds and it is too bright — it's blinding, I'm not kidding. Now behind my closed eyelids I am seeing all sorts of patterns and splotches and those floaty things that bob along between your eyes and your lids. I don't know what they are. I asked the eye doctor once, and he said they were "floaties." I don't think that is a very medical term, frankly. I think he might have made it up.

I can hear the whine of a boat engine out on the water. I wonder if maybe my New Dad is taking the kids out fishing. I want to peek, but I don't. It's like I can't be bothered. That is what I have felt like a lot since the accident — I can barely be bothered to do anything. What do you think that means?

I'm a lazy daisy.

They *are* going fishing; their voices carry over the glassy strait like they are speaking into microphones. I sigh. They didn't even ask me. Not that I would have gone anyway. Maybe I would. Who knows?

I concentrate on the dive in my head. Back somersault with half-twist. I lie on my back and lift my toes up and point them. I hold them like that until my muscles tremble a little. I wish I could practise. But I'm never diving off that rock again. Never.

I can hear Mum's footsteps on the deck, *slip-slapping* in her rubber boots. I close my eyes right away and pretend to be asleep. Sometimes you just don't feel like talking. Blue comes in, and snuggles in beside me. His fur is boiling hot from the sudden sun. This end-of-summer weather can be very odd. Raining one minute, sunny the next. Well, it might be sunny, but how could he be so hot already? It's like the dark brown colour has just sucked in all the heat. I push him away. "You're too hot," I tell him. "Come back when you cool off."

He just looks at me with his big brown eyes,

sort of sadly, like he can see all the way inside me to my broken heart.

Mum pokes her head in and says, "You want some lunch?"

I shake my head. "Not hungry."

"Want to go for a walk on the beach?"

I shrug. And sigh, as if she is asking a lot. Really, I don't think it's a bad idea. You can only lie in a blanket tent for so long. "I guess," I say.

We make our way down the hill, the dogs lolloping along beside us. It's so quiet I can hear the hum of bees flying from thistle flower to thistle flower.

"I wish we could stay here forever," I say.

"Really? Then you wouldn't be able to go back to school, or go to diving, or to gymnastics." She looks at me. "And you wouldn't see your friends."

I shrug. "Whatever."

"Are you okay, Carly?"

"Fine, Mum. Forget it." I mean, she must know that I'm sad about Montana. She knows stuff like that, Mum does. After all, that's her job. I can't even believe she asked me such a stupid question. I'll probably never be okay again.

We walk for a little while in silence. The rocks along the water are all on a slope, so I can feel my ankles and knees pulling with each step. We pass the cave that I used to love when I was little. It's a big hole right in the sandstone. Outside it, there are all these holes in the sandstone that look like footprints. We call them dinosaur footprints, even though I know that's not what they are. I'm old enough to know better. I'm old enough to know about a lot of things: for example, the cave is now the otters' bathroom. I'm not kidding, it stinks. Literally. I think the otters use it as an outhouse, and they poo everywhere. Nothing smells as bad as otter poo. I'm serious. The dogs love it. They roll in it. Talk about disgusting.

Mum is about to say something when I hear this strange sound, sort of like a loud *puff* from the water. We both look over at the same time. It's really loud.

"Look!" says Mum, pointing.

I follow her finger, then I see them. Big black fins rising out of the water.

"Whales!" I say.

We watch as the orcas swim along. One jumps out of the water and slaps back down, making a huge rainbow of spray. We climb up higher so we can see better.

"Oh, my goodness," says Mum.

I look where she is looking and I see the little boat with my New Dad and the kids. It looks very tiny and far away from where we are standing.

"Oh, my goodness," I echo.

The whales get closer to them. I am feeling the little pitter-patter of scared feelings filling up my heart. I can see my New Dad pointing at the whales. Please, God, I pray silently, don't let the whales eat my new family.

I don't usually pray, to tell you the truth. I'm not entirely sure about the whole God situation. Montana's mum prays all the time. When I go to the hospital, she is usually in the chapel, praying. The chapel is this glorified hospital room with a cross and some coloured glass. Also, in Montana's room there is a picture of Jesus Christ. I'm going to ask Mum about church one day. I'm going to ask her what she thinks of the whole thing, about God and Jesus Christ. But not today. I have a lot of stuff to sort out for myself first, in that regard. I never really thought too much about it until Montana's accident, to be honest. But now I've started to think about it. I've started to think that maybe there is someone in charge after all. Why not? I hope there is, anyway. If not, well, I guess we're on our own.

However, I do not want to take any chances. I add Jesus' name to my prayer for good measure.

Anyway, back to Montana's mum: I didn't

understand before why she would be praying instead of sitting with Montana. I do now. It's sort of nice to feel that there is someone in charge, someone you can say to, "Look, please make Montana better." Or in this case, "Please don't let the whales knock the boat over."

The water is about a hundred miles deep where the boat is. Dad waves in sort of a friendly way, so I wave back, even though I am all but having a heart attack. The whales seem to have chosen this exact moment to put on some kind of a show, like you might see at Sea World or something. The scary part is that they are between the boat and the shore. I try to enjoy watching them, but I am much too nervous to relax. I feel a tiny bit like crying.

Finally, after many minutes of leaping about and blow-spitting into the air and slapping their tails, the whales move on. I feel relief come over me like a big wash of water.

"Well," I say. "That's that, then."

Mum grabs my hand. "Scary, huh?" she asks. "But also beautiful."

"I wasn't scared," I lie. I stand up. "What I am is a little uncomfortable." I point to my butt. We were sitting on a rock that was still wet from all the rain, and now my shorts are soaked in a big circle on my rear end. It looks like I peed my pants, like a baby. I was scared, but like I said, not that scared. I knew they'd be okay.

I knew God was looking out for them.

He took away my Real Dad — he couldn't take away my New Dad, too. That just wouldn't be fair.

Dad brings the boat right up to the shore where we are standing.

"Wow," he says. "Did you see the show they put on?"

We nod, and grin, like we think it was fantastic. Marly and Shane are so excited, they are both talking at once.

"Whales!"

"We saw them!"

"Big black whales!"

I say, "You sure were lucky."

I don't want to let on that I was scared for them. They're just little kids. They don't need to worry about stuff like that yet, all the stuff that happens that is bigger than you are. All the stuff that could happen that you can't control at all.

chapter 8

There is something about walking to school on the first day back — the air always seems a few degrees colder, and the knees of your jeans are always stiff and new. I don't know what it is, but there is almost a different smell to the air. Like the sky is full of chalk dust or something. Something cold, like the inside of a skating rink. I am walking by myself. Usually I would walk with Montana, but she isn't coming.

Obviously. Duh.

I kick at the pavement, and stub my toe in my new shoes. The suede gets kind of scuffed, and I'm mad at myself for ruining them before anyone has even seen them yet. This year I will be in Grade Five. Mrs. Whitfield's class. I wonder if we will do anything good this year. Last year, the highlight of the whole entire million months of school was the day we got to go down to the museum and look at the woolly mammoth. That was it. Big excitement.

I get to school, which smells like the hospital, and I start thinking about Montana again, and wondering what she is doing right now. She is probably eating breakfast off one of those trays they bring where everything is covered with its own lid. Or maybe she is in the pool having physiotherapy. That is going to make her muscles strong again, so she can run around and stuff. Of course, her back will be really straight, but other than that she'll be normal.

Did I tell you? We tried the magnet thing. It didn't work at all. I guess there is too much skin and stuff between the metal thing and the magnets. She did say that the doctor told her she would probably set off the alarms at airports when she goes through them. That would be embarrassing, let me tell you. You have to stop and then the police scan your body for guns and knives and things like you are some kind of criminal. I remember that from when we went to Hawaii. It happened to a man in front of me. It turned out it was his belt buckle, which was very big and frankly quite ugly. He was embarrassed and he blushed all over his bald head. I would hate to be bald.

I go right away to the classroom and sort of stand by the window to wait for the other kids to show up. I like the classroom when it's empty and waiting. I imagine that all summer long, this room has been looking forward to this day when it will be all filled up with kids again. It must be so bored during vacation, just collecting dust and spiders.

After school today, I have a private diving lesson with this guy named Bob Brennan. He used to be some really great diver, then he hit his head on the platform. He didn't dive in meets after that, but he does teach kids how to do it. He's a little stricter than Jon, but hopefully he can help me with my tough dive before October. That's when the meet is. It seems like a long time, but it isn't really. Think about it. Four weeks away. It's been twice that long since the hovercraft came and took Montana to the hospital. And that seems like it only just happened yesterday, in some ways. I guess in other ways, it seems like it happened a lifetime ago. All I'm trying to say is that four weeks is not exactly a long time.

Who am I kidding? I'll never be able to pull it off. That Bob Brennan better be some kind of miracle worker. I tell you, my dive is really floppy and loose. I don't know why I can't pull it tighter together. I am usually still in the middle of it when, *bam,* I hit the water. I try to finish it underneath, but I know it isn't right.

I am sitting at a desk, twiddling, because now I am getting nervous about the back somersault with half-twist, and I don't even notice the other kids coming in. Next thing I know, Mrs. Whitfield is there and she is talking and I look beside me and realize I forgot to save a seat for Montana.

I put up my hand.

"Yes?"

"Is this where we are going to sit for all year?" I ask, trying hard not to sound panicky.

"For the time being, dear," she says.

"But . . . "

"Yes?"

"I was going to save a seat for my friend. Montana. She's in the hospital, but I said I would save her a seat. I mean, I promised."

I start to cry a little bit, which is as embarrassing as you can imagine in your worst fears. My face is hot, so it must be bright red. I feel like a baby, then I get mad. I just sit there, scowling.

"Well," she says slowly. "I am sure we can arrange a seat next to you when she comes back."

Then she starts talking again about all the blah blah blah we are going to learn this year. I stare really hard at the scratched initials in my desk, so I don't have to look at the other kids. They must think I'm really stupid and a big baby. I am so embarrassed that I start imagining a giant hole opening up in the floor, and myself doing a back somersault with half-twist right into the centre of the earth.

The bell goes for recess after about a million years, and I think and hope that maybe my face is not so red anymore. All the kids go tearing out into the playground like they are thirsty people in the desert and they have just spotted a puddle of water. Really. I am surprised no one is trampled to death. I go out after them and sit on the fence to watch them play.

A funny-looking girl with braces and black curly hair comes and sits next to me. Finally, she looks over and says, "Montana is my friend, too. I knew her from Sunday school."

"Really?" I eyeball her. "She was my *best* friend. *Is* my best friend," I correct myself quickly.

"Oh. I really like her, too," she says.

"Oh." I don't really know what to say, so I swing my feet back and forth and pretend to kick the bees that are buzzing past.

"How is she?"

"She's okay. She's going to be just fine," I say. "It was an accident, you know."

"I know," she says. "Her mum told my mum. We all pray for her every day."

"Huh," I say. "Great, I'm sure it helps."

I sneak another look at her. She has a kind of funny face, sort of shaped like a heart, but she has splendid hair. Like a doll's hair. Black and super curly in these perfect little ringlets.

"What's your name?" I ask.

"Felicia," she answers.

Felicia! I try to think — is that a good name? I look at her again. Once her teeth are fixed, she is going to be quite pretty, I decide.

"That's a nice name," I tell her. Even though the jury is still out on that one.

"What's your name?" she asks.

"Carly," I tell her. "My sister's name is Marly. Talk about dorky, huh."

"I don't think so," she says. "I like your name."

I guess that's how we come to be friends. Because we both know Montana. It's so funny how one minute you don't know a person, the next you know that their favourite food is macaroni with orange cheese and their favourite sport is soccer and they want to be a mystery writer or a detective when they grow up.

We lie down on the grass by the fence and look up at the clouds. It feels nice. I get a warm feeling in my heart, like maybe things will be okay. We make a daisy chain together. She is going to take it to Montana in the hospital. She is going to say it is a gift from both of us.

After school, my dad picks me up because my mum is working at her new job. She sells fridges and stoves and stuff at a really big store. Anyway, he asks me how my day was, and I tell him all about my new friend and what everyone was wearing and about what Mrs. Whitfield said. He seems to be listening very carefully, and I realize that I am surprised to be telling him. Usually I would just have said, "Fine." Or, "It was okay."

He drops me off at the pool and says he is going to pick Mum up, then they are going to come and watch my lesson.

"Okay," I say. And I think that it's kind of funny, really, that I don't mind. I think it's nice, actually. It makes me feel a bit weird, thinking that, so I don't say anything more. I just get out of the car and slam the door behind me quite hard, and watch him through the window as he shakes his head and makes a fake fist at me. "Don't slam the door!" I can tell he is saying.

Bob is kind of big and scary looking, but he meets me outside the shower and tells me that what we are going to do is to do each dive until I can hardly stand it anymore, until I can do it in my sleep. Between dives, he is going to show me on a video what it looked like, and show me what I am doing wrong, and then I have to do it a million more times until it is perfect.

First thing that happens, I climb up onto the springboard to do my forward somersault dive and I somehow miss completely and belly-flop. Uh-oh. He looks at me and shakes his head and says, "I heard you were a talented diver, but now I'm not so sure."

Huh! That makes me quite mad, I must say. So I march back up onto the board and bounce a couple of times really high and do an absolutely drop-dead-perfect back somersault with half-twist.

Ha! I come to the surface, pushing my hair back out of my eyes, and he is standing there clapping.

"Very good," he says. "Now let's go back to the forward somersault, which is what you were supposed to be doing."

So I do. About a million times. Once I get used to seeing myself on tape without thinking, oh, my hair looks funny when it's wet, or, oh, my face is all bunched up when I hit the water, or, do my legs look really fat when I am jumping, then I can see what I am doing wrong. It helps. I really recommend it. Everyone should tape everything they do, so they can see what they really are. Or, at least, what they look like.

I do so many front somersaults that my head is spinning from going round and round, the ceiling of the pool and the blue, blue water flashing by each time. After forever, we move on to the back somersault. It must be dinnertime, I am thinking; my stomach is growling like mad, like Roo when she sees a raccoon. I don't say anything, though, because I don't want him to think I am a baby. Finally, we move on to the back somersault with half-twist. I am so tired, I can barely climb the ladder, but I manage to pull it off five times. Well, I try it five times, and flub it three times.

Dad comes over from the stands and says, "It's getting late, we have to be going."

"Oh," says Bob. "I didn't notice the time, we were having so much fun. But you're right. We'll see you back here tomorrow, Carly!"

"What?" I say. "Oh?"

"Just kidding," he says. "That's all for this week. You'll be fine!"

He gives me the tape to take home with me.

That night, when I fall into bed, right away in my dream I start diving. And diving and diving and diving and diving . . . which is really quite tiring. By the time I wake up in the morning, I'm good and exhausted, but I don't tell anyone. Because in my dream, all my dives were perfect. I was flying. It felt like magic, and I don't want to talk about it because if I try to explain it, maybe the magic will go away. But if I don't say anything, maybe, just maybe, I'll remember how it felt and I'll be able to do it again. And again.

chapter 9

"Ouch," I snap when Mum pulls my swim cap over my hair. I hate that! It pulls my hair at the roots and I always think that one day I will take it off and all my hair will be inside. It is my new Dolphin Diving Club cap, which matches my Dolphin Diving Club suit just perfectly. Both are dark blue. I am thinking that maybe dark blue will be my new favourite colour. Purple is all very nice, but I think it is more like the favourite colour of a little kid, not a professional diver. I am considering diving as a career. So far, I've come first once and second twice in the meets we had in September. So, ha. I'm obviously very good.

Anyway, the suit looks very glamorous and has *DDC* embroidered on it in white. It fits perfectly, which is important for when you are climbing up and diving because of G.U.B. If you don't know what that stands for, I won't tell you. It has something to do with when your suit is just a teensy bit too small and you climb a ladder in it and then you can't gracefully pull it down when it rides up.

Sam is really nervous and so she is chattering away like a chipmunk who drinks too much coffee. Really. It's almost too much. I am trying not to listen and my mum is fussing with my cap and my straps and stuff. I am singing a song in my head. It is a song that I either made up or heard once on the radio. It is about trying not to cry and keeping your head up at all times and being brave. It is a very pretty song, and I wish I had a better singing voice because then I could sing it out loud and everyone would relax a little. One thing I have noticed is that Sam and I seem to be about the youngest people in this change room. By quite a lot. Or else we are just very short for our age, which I don't believe is true. It is something I might have noticed before now, I'm sure.

Mum kisses me on the cheek and squeezes my hand, so, of course, right away I go to the mirror and rub like crazy to get the lipstick off. What kind of good luck is that? A big red smear on your cheek? She disappears out the door and I look at Sam and she looks really scared, so I say, "We are going to do just great." I'm even more nervous than usual, because I overheard my mum talking on the phone last night and she said, "Carly is going to be in an elite diving meet in the morning." It's something about the word *elite* that is more than a little unnerving. I mean, I'm good at this, but what if I'm not *elite*? Quite probably, it is not elite to belly-flop off the board, or fall off the ladder, or hit your head on the bottom. I'm thinking that all of these things are possible. But I take a deep breath and try to force myself to stay calm.

The big clock above the showers shows the exact time to be 8:50. So that's it. Ten minutes and then we will all be out there, diving our heads off. I take another deep breath and this time I hold it until my eyes go blurry, and then off we go out to meet Jon and Bob, who are standing around by the pool.

It happens really fast. I'm telling you, it's amazing. One minute, it's 8:50; the next, I am climbing up the ladder, feeling the familiar cold wet metal with my hands and feet, and I am looking out into the crowd. I can see my mum and dad waving, and both the kids are wearing Dolphin Diving Club sweatshirts and are grinning like mad monkeys. I feel very floaty and funny like I can't quite feel my knees or feet, but I know I am moving because the board wobbles as I walk to the end. I spring up and down for a minute at the end and there is total silence. Completely. I'm not kidding, it's amazing. This is nothing like the meets that I am used to. For one thing, the stands are jam-packed with people. And for another, the judges look very serious and intimidating. I swallow hard to pull myself together. And I just float up into the ceiling and stay there for a minute, and then plop into the pool. It is sharp and clean, with no splash. Perfect! My heart is going *plippity-clippity* and I hoist myself out of the pool with no effort at all. Bob grins and Jon gives me the thumbs-up.

I did it!

It is a whirlwind. Sam does her dive and then the other kids go, and then it is my turn again. It all happens very fast. Finally, it is Sam's last dive and I try to watch, but to tell you the truth, I can't really concentrate because I look out into the crowd and you won't believe who is there. I'm serious.

Guess.

No?

It's *Montana*. She is right there with her mum and she is waving and her hair is tied up on top with a big blue bow. Well, there is a big blue bow around her head, anyway, kind of like a head-band. Her hair is not quite long enough for an actual bow. But it is growing amazingly fast.

I start right away to feel guilty that I am diving and she isn't, but I wave at her anyway and point her out to Sam and we wave and wave from the entrance to the change room. She sees us and waves back, and just for a minute everything seems almost normal.

I guess I am a little distracted, because my next-to-last dive is so bad I can barely tell you about it. It's awful. It is the worst dive at the whole meet and no one even claps when I hit the water — there is just this silence and I can hear some people coughing and stuff. Really, they could have been nice about it. What kind of people are they?

Then I notice that Marly and Shane are clapping and yelling, so I feel a little better. Not much, but a little. I guess that everyone makes mistakes, don't they? I think the crowd is quite mean to not at least applaud sympathetically. Give me a break. I feel really bad. Actually, I feel bad and mad, both. Frankly, I am slightly mad at Montana for showing up unannounced and making me nervous. I mean, it's bad enough that I feel about a metre shorter and ten years younger than everyone else, even though I know that can't be true. After all, this is the "eleven-and-under" category. Well, everyone else must be practically twelve, or lying about their age. Or maybe I can expect to grow a lot in the next few months. Anway, I'm so upset that I go right into the change room and cry. I'm not proud, but it's true. I am a failure. I will never be a diver. Obviously, I'm not good enough for an elite meet, and so I'm never going to be good enough for the Olympics. I'll just have to do something else. *Phhhffit*. I'll probably just sell fridges and stoves, like my mum. Or maybe I'll go live at the cabin forever. Then I won't need to have a job.

I sit there for a long time and watch the green second hand race around the clock. Why do they have a lap-timer clock in the change room? So you can time your shower? It's ridiculous. I hate it that someone would be so stupid to put that clock in here.

A bunch of the older girls are getting changed and their hairspray is filling up the air with chemicals and I feel like I can't breathe. They all have brought their own hair dryers so that they don't have to bend over and try to dry their hair under those ridiculous air nozzles. I should have thought of that. What kind of baby am I? I never thought I could bring my own.

I watch them for a while, then I drag myself off the bench, where I have been sitting for so long that there are little dents on the backs of my legs. It looks like I have been walloped. Really. I slump back into the pool area and I realize that I am up next and I am expected to do the back somersault with half-twist dive. I couldn't even do the backward tuck! What are they thinking? But they are calling my number, so I go up to the springboard and climb and climb and climb and finally I am at the top and I look out directly at Montana. She is sitting next to Felicia, my new friend, and they both hold up their crossed fingers and smile a little bit. Right away, I say out loud to myself in a whisper, "I am going to do this for Montana."

I am going to do a perfect back somersault with half-twist.

I am.

I . . .

hear the board *thwack* under my feet and I close my eyes and concentrate really hard on Montana and pretend I am her with my black silky hair flying around my face and I do a somersault and

a twist . . .

and there is still so much time before I hit the water.

I did it!

I come up and I can hear the clapping and it is

amazing! I did it! Jon comes over and hugs me, which is pretty nice. If you know what I mean.

I knew I won, right away. Even though I flubbed one of my dives. I guess everyone gets to make one mistake.

I won.

My heart is trumpeting! *Pa-pum! Pa-pum!* I swear that I am actually walking on air. I go put on my new DDC sweatshirt and jogging pants and wait around with the other girls for the ceremony. I have taken off my cap and slicked back my hair and I think I look pretty good in the pictures. I look like I belong there. Sam won two medals, but hers are silver. I got one and it's gold. Well, they aren't real. Obviously. They are plastic, on shiny ribbons, but they feel real enough to me. It's not like I was going to use it for money or anything. I think that one gold medal might be just a bit more impressive than two silver ones, but I would never tell Sam that. No way. Besides, she was brave enough to dive from the tower, so she deserves that second medal more than me.

Afterwards, I find Montana in the crowd. She is really excited. She keeps clapping her hands and saying, "I can't believe you won! You were so incredible!" And I think about all the reasons why she is my best friend ever; even though I really like Sam and Felicia, it just isn't the same.

So I take the medal and I hang it around her neck. It looks perfect on her. Like that's where it belonged the whole time.

"Wow," she says.

"Wow," I say.

Then she does this thing that is really amazing. She stands up from her wheelchair and hugs me really hard. So hard that tears come to my eyes. From the hugging, I'm sure. She can stand up! Then she tells me that she has been walking around, too, and that she is getting much better. So much better that she doesn't really need to use the chair very much at all.

It's going to be okay, I hear this voice in my head say. She's going to be okay. I can't believe it. It's better than a gold medal. It's better than a million gold medals.

I say, "Next year we'll find some real gold at the cabin if you still are allowed to come with me. I made a map," I add. "I think we'll probably find the treasure."

"Really?" she says, and her dark eyes are all sparkly like wet rocks or seal's eyes.

And so I say, "Yeah, really. Of course, *really*."

Sam grins and tells Felicia all about it, about

Brother XII and the gold that he hid on the island. Felicia looks thrilled. Thrilled to be included or thrilled about the gold, I don't know which. I feel all warm inside, suddenly, like a whoosh of hot happiness has just filled me right up. I squeeze Montana's hand and it feels like a normal hand and everything feels just right. It is warm here in the stands — even though it is raining outside and cold and windy — and smells of chlorine and popcorn and we are all friends and the medal sparkles in the lights over Montana's sweatshirt.

I sit with her for a long time. All of us together. Sam and Montana and Felicia and me. We sit and watch the rest of the meet and we share a big plate of nachos and fake cheese. And Mum waves but doesn't make me go sit with them, my whole family.

It's perfect.

Really.

I never knew it was possible to be this happy. My heart is singing and floating and puffing away like one of those whales at the cabin.

I feel free.

chapter 10

So that's the story. The whole thing that happened last year.

Montana is getting better really fast. She has to have another operation after she has finished growing, but she can almost walk normally now. You would never know that she had some parts to her that weren't real. Even her hair is getting longer again. She is taking flute lessons now, too, to make up for the fact she can't do gymnastics and diving. Also, she is swimming. She likes it, she told me. She is getting really strong. Actually, she can swim way faster than me. I don't let it bother me, though. I don't let that kind of stuff come into my head at all anymore.

That's my New Year's resolution.

Whenever I have a thought like that coming on, I give my head a shake, like Roo and Blue do when there is water in their ears from swimming. I shake my head really hard and get rid of all of those who-is-better-than-who thoughts.

There was just one more thing I wanted to say now. I said I wasn't going to talk about my Real Dad, but I am, just for a minute. See, Montana told me that when she dove in and hit her head on the sunken log and just kind of stayed down there at the bottom, she opened her eyes and looked around down there and she says it was incredibly, amazingly beautiful. She says the water was really green and a big school of silver fish swam by her and she says it was very peaceful. Really. I'm just repeating what she told me. She said, "I thought I had died and that it was heaven and then I realized I couldn't breathe."

Wow, huh.

So she says she got a bit panicky and then all of a sudden got this really happy feeling, not like happy happy, but more like joyous. Like singing in church. And she says it was really calm and warm and she wasn't scared at all.

After that, I guess my dad — my New Dad, that is, but I don't call him that anymore — anyway, he saved her, and we all know what happened after that. Somehow, it got me to thinking a bit about my Real Dad.

You see, he was driving in his car and it slipped off an icy bridge and into a river. He was in Ontario at the time. I guess it's pretty cold there and there are more bridges and slippery roads. So the point is that he drowned in his car, which is funny, but not like funny ha-ha, more like funny sad. I have been thinking that maybe that is what it was like for him. Sort of peaceful and warm and not cold and scary like I had originally thought. I think maybe he felt joyous, too, a little bit. Even though he wasn't one for going to church, let me tell you. He knew what it was like, though. Everyone knows that feeling, of everyone singing in a big group and your heart just lifting and lifting and lifting until it gets to be part of the sky and the clouds and the sun and the moon and everything.

That's where my Real Dad is.

So, I'm okay.

Really.

Montana, Felicia, Sam and I have made a club of our own. It's called the GDC, which stands for Gold Diggers Club. Don't tell anyone. It's a secret. Next summer, we are going to find that treasure. We are going to find that treasure and all that gold and then we will be so rich we won't know what to do with ourselves. Montana is such a nice person she is going to buy plane tickets for her parents to go home to the Philippines and bring back everyone in her family. She has about a hundred cousins there. Plus two grandmas and two grandpas. Felicia is going to buy a really big house. Sam is torn between buying a CD player and putting the money in the bank. I think I will buy my family some things, too. I can be a nice person. I will buy Marly her own purple house so she doesn't have to share my room on weekends. Ha! I'm teasing. She's not so bad anymore. She's okay.

This is what I'm going to do: I am going to buy my own pool. I am going to buy a bunch of diving boards and I am going to dive all day long and all night and then, after that, later or when I'm grown-up, I'm going to the Olympics.

I think I can probably win. I just have to feel it.

I have to feel the gold-medal dive.

I can't wait till next summer. I can't wait to find that treasure.

Turn the page for a preview of the next book
about Carly, *Barely Hanging On.*

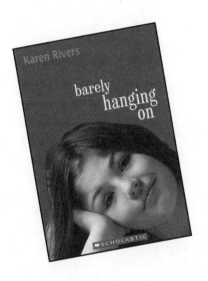

chapter 1

This has started out to be practically the worst day in the world. I'm not kidding. For one thing, last night I had the most horrible dream ever. It was about my mum. My mum is having a baby. In real life, not just in the dream. The baby won't come until July, and it's only February. I *know* that, okay? But in dream-time that doesn't make any difference. In the dream she was having the baby, like today. Her belly was huge, bigger than a basketball or a beachball or any kind of ball. I mean it. It was enormous. In real life, it is still just a tiny bulge, but in the dream she was gigantic. She looked barely like a person! Particularly considering that she had very small, beady eyes, like rat's eyes or something even more awful than that. If I were going to be honest here, I'd say she didn't look much like my mum at all, more like an especially large and unfriendly rodent. Somehow I knew it was my mum though, in the way that you know things in dreams. Which was weird because my mum is really very pretty. I don't look anything like her. She has long blond hair and perfect teeth. My hair isn't blond and my teeth are very small and spaced apart. They look like the teeth of a much smaller person or a baby. It isn't good. I don't even think they can fix the kind of teeth that I have, unless there are some kind of braces that make your teeth bigger.

Anyway, in the dream I was shivering cold (probably my window was open in real life; I like the window open when I sleep so that I can breathe fresh air) and there was snow all around. We were walking through a big field and there was no one else there and it was really creepily quiet. I could hear the snow crunching under our shoes. I only sort of knew it was a dream, if you know what I mean. It did snow yesterday, so the whole snow thing made it feel kind of real. Then all of a sudden Mum-monster said, "Oh Carly, your sister's coming," and out of her snowsuit popped this fully-grown little girl the same size as me, only she had skin like a snake and her eyes were red and flashing. I screamed and screamed. I mean, I really did scream. I screamed so loud that I came out of the dream and woke up and I was standing on my bed and Mum and my New Dad were standing there staring at me like I was some kind of alien creature. Me! Huh. I tried to explain to them about the dream, but dreams are hard to tell to other people. They never sound as scary when you say them out loud, and sometimes they sound even a little bit funny. I could see my mum try not to laugh a bit when I got to the part about the lizard skin. Really. That isn't very nice, I'm sure you'll agree.

Dad (I call him Dad, even though he isn't my Real Dad) made me some hot soy milk and stayed up with me for a little while, but he couldn't stop yawning. Mum fell asleep on my bed. She snores. This isn't her prettiest quality, I can tell you that. I hope I don't snore, but how would I know for sure? Finally Dad went back to bed in his own room. I turned off the light, but all the shadows started to look like the Reptile Girl, so I turned it back on. Mum didn't wake up, which is good, because she is very grouchy when she gets woken up unexpectedly. Luckily, she can sleep through almost anything. She says that her body is making a baby and it uses up a lot of energy, so she needs her rest. I suppose that must be true.

I can't imagine why she wants another baby. After all, she has me. I'm Carly. I'm ten going on eleven. By the time this baby is my age, I'll be twenty-one! I'll be an adult. I'll be old enough to have kids of my own! And she'll just be a kid. Or he. Whatever. Also, as far as kids go, my mum has Marly, who is five, and Shane, who is almost three. That seems like more than enough, even though Marly and Shane aren't really hers. They came with my New Dad. A complete package. The only thing he didn't bring along was a dog, which is good because we already have two dogs. We have Roo, who was my Real Dad's dog, and I have a dog of my very own called Blue. The rhyming names were a joke. Like Carly and Marly. Which is also a joke, but not that funny.

My full name is Carly Abbott-Fitzgerald. The Fitzgerald is new. On Christmas I told my New Dad that I would take his last name. It sounds kind of weird, but my last name was Abbott and when Mum married my New Dad, she took his name, which is Fitzgerald, but I didn't want to do that. People called me that because they didn't know, or whatever, but I didn't change it officially. I mean, I already had a perfectly good name. My Real Dad's name. He died, but that doesn't change anything. I was the only one in the family with a different name. Then all of a sudden I decided I didn't always want to be the different one, so I tacked the

Fitzgerald onto the end of my name. Who knew you could do that? Now I'm Carly Abbott-Fitzgerald on paper. It was totally a big deal, but really it's quite meaningless. I mean, in real life I'm still just me, Carly. Nothing is different. My new name is quite a bit more glamorous than the real me. I like it though. Perhaps I will grow into it. It sounds like the name of a movie star or a super-model or even a gold-medal-winning athlete.

My mum snored all the rest of the night and I couldn't get back to sleep, so I read a book for an hour or two and then my alarm went off. The book was *Little Women*, in case you were wondering. It is both good and not good. I get tired of the way they are always dressing up and fussing with their hair and blah, blah, blah, but I like to read it. I like Jo. She is tough and I imagine if it had been an option for her at the time, she would have enjoyed diving as much as I do.

I should tell you that I'm hoping to be an Olympic diver when I grow up. Probably by the time my new sister/brother is my age, in fact. That's kind of neat to think about. I didn't realize that until just now. I'll have to remember to tell Mum that later. I'm sure she'll be excited. What she has thought of (and tells everyone who asks) is that I'll be just the right age to babysit the new baby for free. Ha! That's funny. If I'm going to be babysitting anyone, I will demand to be paid. A lot. I don't babysit Marly and Shane because I'm too young. You have to be twelve to babysit for some reason. Not that I would want to look after those two. That would be a handful, I'm sure. I barely like spending the weekend with them, to tell you the honest truth. They are just here on weekends most of the time, because they have a mother and she has them the rest of the time. We have them for all this month, though, because their mother is away in Australia, which I am quite jealous about. Who goes to Australia? It is a million miles away from here. I want to go to Australia very badly. I've seen it on TV and it looks very nice and hot and the animals are much more interesting than ours and also there are a lot of terrific divers from Australia. The Olympics were there once. There is a lot of money there for sports, or so Dad tells me.

It is now sometime in the afternoon and I am at school and I'm tired and frankly I'm in no mood for today. Also, not being able to sleep has affected my hair and it is sticking out all over the place and little wisps of it keep floating by my eyes to remind me how gross it is. I feel ugly and mad. So there. And today is a stupid day. Do you want to know what day it is? Well, you can guess. It's the stupidest day of the year.

Yes indeedy, it's stupid *Valentine's* Day. Yuck.

I don't know who invented such a stupid day, but my teacher, whose name is Mrs. Whitfield (although I like to call her Mrs. Witless because she has no sense of humour whatsoever and is always yelling at me), decided that everyone had to make a stupid valentine for another person in the class, and that person had to be someone who was not your friend. For example, if you are a girl, the card has to be for a boy. You can imagine how much fun this is, can't you? So I made my stupid card, and I gave it to this boy named Tim because I think he is cute. A bit cute, not a lot. He dives with me in the Dolphin Diving Club. He is pretty good, but not that good. I used to think he was pretty good. I should say, used to, as in, not any-more. I also used to think he was cute. Now I know he is not cute or even slightly nice.

This is what happened: I made a nice, beautiful card with hearts made of tissue paper and very delicate little Kleenex flowers and . . . I kid you not . . . he opened it and laughed at it and held it up to the light. It was a little wispy, I grant you that, because it was so *delicate*. And then he BLEW HIS NOSE ON IT. He says he thought it was a Kleenex.

I am so mad that I could spit. To make it even worse, the only boy who gave me a valentine was this weird kid named Smith. Smith has braces and his hair is so white it is almost non-existent. From a distance it is the same colour as his white skin, so it just looks like a bald head. Baldness freaks me out. His card was very nice, though. Very artistic and also funny. Not that it makes it less humiliating to get a card from him. I mean, really. Smith!

And to make it even worse, that stupid Tim, who I *used* to think was cute, made a big red and purple card for my best friend Montana. Montana got six cards. Huh! What am I supposed to think? I love Montana. And I mean love in the way that you love your family kind of love. Not girl-boy kind of love. Duh. Obviously. Montana is my best friend in the world, but sometimes I hate her a little bit because she is totally beautiful. She is beautiful *and* nice *and* smart *and* brave. Something horrible happened last year, which I will tell you quickly so that you know, if you don't know already.

It happened when we were diving off rocks at my cabin. My cabin is on an island near here, but to get there you have to take a boat. Sometimes I am allowed to bring friends, and on this weekend

I was allowed to bring two friends because Mealy Marly and Shane were away. So me and Montana and Sam (my best friend from diving club) were practising our dives into the water, which was dark and blackish-green. Well, not really. It was just regular water, but when you stood on the rock and looked in, it looked like it was green. You couldn't see the bottom. I guess there was stuff down there that we didn't know about. Obviously. How could we have known? Montana dove into a sunken log and broke her back. It was super scary, in a very bad way. When I tell it quickly, it doesn't seem so bad, but trust me, it was. To make it worse, when she was in the hospital, they cut off all her hair. Which you would think would make her less perfectly gorgeous. But instead she now has it in a really cute pixie cut and she looks better than ever. Really, I'm very happy about it. I am. She is almost completely patched up from the accident, although she doesn't dive anymore because part of her back doesn't bend — it has a steel rod in it — and sometimes she gets tired faster than the rest of us, but she is almost back to her normal self. I don't want you to think I am a horrible person for being a tiny bit jealous about the valentines. Actually, I'm not jealous at all, I've decided. After all, who wants a stupid valentine from stupid Tim, the Nose Blower?

Not that I care, but Felicia, who is our other friend in this class, got three cards. She is not perfectly gorgeous like Montana but she is funny and smart. What is wrong with me? I am just Little Miss Unpopular. I don't know why. I'm a nice girl! I smile at people! Mum always says it doesn't matter what you look like, as long as you smile a lot. I do smile a lot. I find a lot of things funny, for Pete's sake. All that smiling should have got me at least two cards. Oh, forget it. Obviously, I am repellant to boys and will spend the rest of my life alone. That's just fine because I am a very busy person and don't have time to worry about boys and all that other stuff. I have a lot going on. On Saturdays and Wednesdays, I have diving practice first thing in the morning, at, like, six o'clock. It is very important to get up at the very crack of dawn to practise, because then you feel like you are really sacrificing something for your sport. In this case, the sacrifice is sleeping. I'm all for sleeping, but I'd rather dive. Besides, when I get famous they will do a TV show about me and I need to be able to say how early I used to get up, and Mum and Dad will need to talk about how they never had to wake me because I was always awake because I was so excited about practice. This isn't always entirely true, but I will coach them to say it on the TV special, when there is one.

So you see that I am very busy. Also, I take gymnastics after school on Tuesdays and Fridays. On Wednesdays, I take my not-really-my-sister Marly to piano lessons and then take her home to her mum's house on the bus. My mum says this is a good experience for me with responsibility, but the truth is that she works until four o'clock on Wednesdays and Dad works until five. So you can see how this works. I can do this not-so-fun job, but I can't babysit for money. Whatever. I like the bus. I always meet super-interesting people on the bus. Once I met a man who claimed to be Jesus Christ. I don't think he really was. Well, clearly, he wasn't. But he looked the part, what with the beard and wild hair.

On Mondays, I play at Montana's house, or Felicia's house, or Sam's house. I only tell you all this so you see how full my weeks are. I have no time for boys! I don't care about valentines. Not at all. I glare at Smith until he blushes, which is about ten seconds because he has thinner skin than me and blushes very easily. I feel a little bit mean, but I don't care because I'm in a bad mood. If I grow up and marry Smith we will have pale children with bad hair, which cannot happen. I feel bad about glaring but the sooner he knows, the better. I don't want this to get out of hand.

I decide to spend the rest of the afternoon carving my name into my desk with my compass from my geometry set. The compass, I'm sure you'll agree, isn't good for much else, except for drawing perfect circles. But only if you want to draw a circle with a hole in the middle. One thing that works to avoid this is to stick the pin part in an eraser first and then spin it around while it is stuck in the eraser. It is harder to make a perfect circle this way though, because the eraser sometimes moves. Well, you try it. You'll see what I mean.

I'm very good at carving on my desk without getting caught. It's an art, as Dad would say. He says everything is an art, when it clearly isn't. I don't get it, but I say it all the time. I can't help it. He must influence me more than he thinks. I carve all through Science and partway into Math, which was the second-to-last class of the day, when something horribly embarrassing happens. I don't even want to tell you what.

Oh, forget it. I'll just tell you then, and you'll laugh and laugh, but it isn't funny and it hurt. Okay. Don't read this if you don't like gory stories! Don't say I didn't warn you!

I was carving away, very quietly — *scrape,*

scrape, scrape — when the compass *slipped from my hand* and I *stabbed* it into the fat part of my other hand at the bottom of my thumb. Not gently, either. I was working on the curlicue part at the bottom of the *y* of my name. I was pressing quite hard! The stupid compass skidded and jammed into my thumb and got stuck. To be honest, I might have screamed. At least, I mumbled, "Help! Help!" Finally someone noticed, and Mrs. Whitfield came over and pulled it out and there was a big sploosh of blood and I *fainted*. I'm not kidding. First she was there, and then the room went all grey and the next thing I knew I was opening my eyes and my head was hanging upside down and everyone was staring at me.

I'll probably never live this down.

I have to get a shot, like right away, so that I don't get tetanus, which is a fatal and terrible disease. The shot hurts also, but not as much as the whole compass situation. I wonder if that's what it feels like to pierce your ears. If so, I'm sure I don't want anything to do with it. I'm allowed to get my ears pierced when I am eleven, which is coming up soon, so this is something I've been thinking about a great deal.

After the shot, I lie down in the nurse's room for several minutes and contemplate my total humil-

iation. It is quite possible that I will die of embar-
rassment if I have to go back to class. I decide that
I will stay here in the nurse's room until after
school, and then I will sneak quietly away. This is
a great room. The nurse is very nice and lets me
do an eye test and a hearing test. I pass both of
those much more easily than I pass most tests.
She also lets me take my temperature and stuff.
This is fun. Well, it isn't really fun, but it's much
better than going back to class.

"You have a lovely office," I tell her. I am trying
to have an adult conversation.

"Uh, thanks," she says. She keeps looking at
the phone. When it rings, she practically leaps on
it. She must have a very interesting life, and the
phone call is probably from her gorgeous boyfriend. She giggles a bit into the phone, which is
somewhat disconcerting. I mean, she's the nurse.
I can tell she doesn't want me to listen, so I go
look out her window. This office has big windows,
and it is a nice-ish day outside because it snowed
yesterday and today it is sunny, so everything
looks very bright and clean and fresh. Probably
the snow is melting though, and what looks nice
and fresh from here is actually slush. I hate slush.
It is the absolute worst. It is useless for snowballs
and snowmen and does not crunch under your

feet like proper snow. It has no point. It is just like very wet, very cold puddles. I have to walk home today, too, which is not nice. I should get rides at least on days when it snows. It hardly ever snows here. Once or twice a year at the most. The snow-fall yesterday was quite a surprise. I took the kids outside and we made snow forts. It was perfect building snow. Not today. Like I said, today it's just slush and *blech.*

The nurse is on the phone for ages and I'm getting bored. This day is not improving. I hate to imagine what else will happen. So far, there has been the Valentine Fiasco and the Compass Stabbing. When she finally hangs up, I lie down on the green vinyl couch and start asking questions. Her name is Stephanie and she is from Quebec. I have never met anyone from Quebec before. She says she speaks French but she has no accent at all. She says people speak both languages in Quebec, and she spoke mostly English. I'm not sure that could be true. Sometimes I watch the French channel and it is all French, all the time. I don't understand a word of it. Which is funny, because I do speak a bit of French. Well, not really. I can say, "Where is the bathroom?" (*"Où est la salle de bain?"*) but that's about all. Finally, after an hour, she says, "Carly, I think you'll be just fine, you should probably head back." Secretly, I think she is just annoyed by my questions. I am very interested in other people, and sometimes I ask them too much and they get short with me. Stephanie was getting a little short, so I knew it was over.

So I go back to class.

I take the long way, up the stairs and down the other stairs and around the outside bike racks — there are only about ten bikes because who rides their bike in the snow? — and back through the door by the gym where the little kids are playing some weird game that involves flags and balls. It looks kind of fun, so I watch through the window for a while, and then I realize that it's freezing outside and I don't have a jacket. I wish I did, because then I could stay out here for longer, but I'm cold as anything so I go in.

I slide into my seat and I'm blushing like mad, so I keep my head down. I blush easily, though not as easily as Smith. I like to think that I blush "prettily." Amy is always "blushing prettily" in *Little Women*. I guess this is a situation where anyone would blush. Montana passes me a note that says, *Are you okay?* I just nod really fast and I don't look at her because I feel so stupid. I try to concentrate on what Mrs. Whitfield is blah, blah, blahing about, and it turns out she is assigning us a project to do in groups of three about something historical that happened around here, such as the Gold Rush or whatever. We can pick what we want to do, but we have to write a paper and do a presentation about it. Yuck! Horrible-ness!

We get to talk about our project for the last fifteen minutes of school, so naturally my "group" will be Montana and Felicia and instead of talking about *that* we talk about what it felt like to pass out and I let them peek under my Band-Aid at the hole made by the stupid compass and I show them the mark from the needle. We giggle about the valentines for a bit and finally the bell goes and it's time to go home.

It's Tuesday, so I only get to go home for an hour and have something to eat such as fruit or raw vegetables, and then I go to gymnastics. I would much prefer to have a cookie or some cake or something but my mum is a health-food freak suddenly. Particularly since she got pregnant. I'm lucky to get granola on a good day. It takes about ten minutes to walk home, and the slush is wet and soaks into my pants. My mood is bad. Basically I am very, very mad because the day was so horrible, so I am stomping into puddles and getting mud all over myself. Which makes me madder. I don't care. I'm sure I'll get in trouble and that will just cap off this day to perfection.

I get home and try the door and it's locked, which is wonderful because I don't have a key. Who locks their own kid out of the house? This is insane! I have to go to the bathroom so badly I will probably pee my pants. How could the house be locked? This is a horrible, crazy joke, clearly. I ring the doorbell and the dogs bark so I talk to them through the glass, but no one opens it.

"Roo," I say. "Let me in!" She kind of barks again in a howly sort of way and paws the glass blocks on her side. That's all very well, but it doesn't open the door.

Where could they all be? I go look for the car in the driveway and it isn't there. Immediately, I get to feeling a little worried. Maybe it isn't Tuesday, maybe it's Monday and I'm supposed to be some-where else. Have I got it all mixed up? I'm only ten; I'm much too young to start forgetting things. Mum forgets things sometimes; she says it's "pregnant brain," which means, I guess, that pregnancy makes you forgetful. Maybe she forgot that today was Tuesday and went somewhere, accidentally thinking that I was going somewhere else. I don't know quite what to do. I could try to climb in a window, but I can't open them. A win-dow up high is open a bit, but I can't see how I can reach it without a ladder. We don't have a ladder.

I sit on the stoop, which is covered with a bit of wet, half-melted snow. It's very, very cold as it seeps slowly through my pants, but I'm too upset to move. It looks like I wet my pants, which I didn't, although I'm not far from it. I put my head in my hands. I'm practising making my super-annoyed face so that when Mum pulls into the driveway and is all apologetic and stuff then I can pretend to be really mad instead of relieved, which frankly I would be if she showed up. I'm going to be late for gymnastics and won't have time to eat my celery or whatever today's treat might be.

I am there for maybe ten minutes when Mr. Taft from across the street comes running over. I can see his face and I start to feel really panicky, like I might faint again, because he has this really alarmed look.

"Carly!" he says, "I'm sorry, I was planning to be here to let you in!"

This is very weird, because I've barely ever talked to him and he's never let me into my own house before. So I say, "Why's that?"

And he says, "It's your mum, Carly, she had to go to the hospital, it's the baby." And I swear, I just about faint again. I sit down really hard and probably bruise my bottom very badly and tears come to my eyes, but I'm not really crying.

He says very quickly, "She's fine though, it's okay, Carly, really, she's fine, she wanted me to tell you that she'll be home in an hour and it was a false alarm. Carly, don't cry!" He kind of half-hugs me and pulls me upright and takes me inside, and he makes me the most delicious hot chocolate I've ever had. I didn't even know we had the stuff for hot chocolate. Is this soy? It's amazing. It tastes like hot, melted chocolate ice cream. And finally, I start to calm down a little bit and I tell him about fainting at school. He's very funny about it and makes me giggle. I never knew he was funny. He was just Mr. Taft-with-the-perfect-lawn before. Now I know much more about him. For instance, he used to be a professional golfer. He was on TV. He played all over the world and won money if he played well. If he didn't, he didn't get paid. Now he teaches golf at the golf course up the street. He lights up when he talks about golf. He must love it like I love diving. Perhaps that's why his lawn is so perfect — it's like a golf course. He is going to teach me to play golf one day, maybe, if I have time. I tell him I have a lot of other stuff going on, such as diving and so on, and may not ever have time. But he doesn't seem that upset. Really, he is very nice about it.

Finally, after an hour or more, I hear the car in

the driveway and I start to feel scared again, so I run out to meet Mum and Dad. They have Marly and Shane with them, which seems a little unfair as I have been home by myself and worried sick and they are all happy and not worried. It isn't fair. But I don't even make a Big Deal of it because I'm so happy to see Mum and Dad. Usually, I am happy to make a Big Deal when it comes to Mealy Marly and Shane. Today, I am almost glad to see them. Well, not really.

I get snow and slush all over my bare feet, which is kind of fun, particularly seeing as I can go right back inside and warm them up. There are hugs all around and we all pile into the kitchen. Mr. Taft goes home. Mum tells me that she just had a tummyache and thought it was something to do with the baby. Well I guess it was, in a way, and what it means is that she has to stop working, for one thing. She is an appliance salesperson, in that she sells fridges and stoves and so on and is on her feet all day. But no more of that! She has to lie down a lot until the baby is born, and some person named Nanny is going to move into our house for a while and work here full-time helping out and stuff. This is also good news because there is always the possibility that this Nanny will cook things like hamburgers and fried chicken which we normally would never get to eat unless they were made of tofu. Maybe Nanny will also be nicer than Mum, who I don't mind telling you is turning into a bit of a grouch. The bad part of it is that the new room that Dad built downstairs, which was going to be my new room when the baby comes, will be this Nanny's room while she is living with us. That isn't fair, but I can see this isn't a good time to argue about it, and I'm just happy Mum's okay.

Fine, that isn't true, the truth is that I said, "But that's my room, she can't have my room!"

And Mum said, "It's just for a little while."

And I said, "No way!" And then I said, "I hate you and this stupid baby!" I just added that last part for a dramatic flair. I didn't mean for it to be so, well, mean.

And then Mum said, "Carly, for God's sake, I really don't want to deal with this kind of nonsense from you right now."

"Why not?" I said, "Because it's something about me for a change and not about the stupid new baby."

And she started to say something, but instead she kind of made a coughing sound and *burst into tears.* Of course, I felt horrible, so I said that this Nanny-person could have my room after all and that it was fine. It isn't really fine. I was looking forward to that room. I was going to paint the walls this super pale purple colour that I had already picked out. Also, it is bigger than my current room. We were going to choose the carpet this weekend. But I hate seeing my mum cry. There is nothing worse. I guess that she had a pretty bad day and didn't need for me to make it worse. So I let it go. See, I can be nice, right?

But I'm still mad about the room.

We end up ordering a pizza and watching movies, which is something that never happens on a school night. I miss gymnastics altogether, but Mum says that's okay because tonight is a special family night where we get to celebrate that we're a family and that my little brother/sister is okay. It's not that much of a celebration because Marly gets a stomach ache from eating cheese and starts having a big, huge temper tantrum. Shane tries to hug her to make it better and she pushes him and he nearly falls down the stairs. Those two can be really annoying. My stomach kind of hurts, too, because I'm not used to eating things that taste like anything other than cardboard. But you don't see me pushing anyone down the stairs, do you?

And that is the end of my horrible, stupid day.